DANCING
feet

VERONICA HELEY

DANCING
feet

Scripture Union
130 City Road, London EC1V 2NJ.

By the same author
Swift Books
Sky High

Leopard Books
Hawkeye of Paradise Row
The Paradise Row Gang
Hawkeye hits the Jackpot

Tiger Books
Good for Kate!

For 6–8s
Natasha's Badge
Natasha's Swing
Natasha the Brownie

© Veronica Heley 1991

First published 1991

ISBN 0 86201 704 1

Phototypeset by Input Typesetting Ltd, London
Printed and bound in Great Britain by Cox and Wyman Ltd, Reading.

To
Number 2 Babe, Charlotte Webb
and
Madame Petrina Tate
who helped me write this story

Chapter One

Pippa was happy for one and three quarter hours every week.

'Rise up! Two, three! Turn! Two, three! Down! Two, three! No, no, Carol, your right arm looks like a dead twig! Think what you are doing. Gracefully, like this . . .'

Madame demonstrated, her body twisting to the music with all the grace which poor Carol lacked. Carol was ten years old, and Madame was – well, who would dare to ask Madame how old she was?

Pippa hadn't understood why Madame had a French name when she was British, but her friend Vibeke had told her that nearly all dancing teachers were called Madame. It was traditional, said Vibeke. Besides, the title 'Madame' suited her.

Madame was like no-one else Pippa knew. Her hair was white, but it was stylishly cut and her skin was young and smooth. She wouldn't have been seen dead in dowdy clothes. Today she wore an emerald green track suit and navy leg-warmers above her ballet shoes. Madame's voice might crack with rage or enthusiasm, but she could still kick higher and faster than anyone in the class. Madame was something else!

'Now try it again, from the beginning. Pippa, come out to the front. Carol can watch you, and maybe then she'll get it right. Up, two three. Turn, two three. . . .'

Pippa went up on her toes with her arms lifted above her head, and turned, letting her arms fall into a graceful downward curve, and down, two three . . .

She had practised this exercise at home so often that she could rise up on her toes without effort. She watched her arms. Her left ankle felt a little stiff, and she knew it didn't make quite such a good line as the right one. She must work on that.

'Right! And relax. You can all take a short break.'

The class broke up, chattering, laughing, complaining of a difficult move. They were all dressed in royal blue, either in leotards, or dance costumes with tiny skirts. Some of them wore loose blue trousers and ankle-warmers, too. Pippa flexed that awkward left ankle of hers. Again, and again. And again. It just would not behave as she wanted it to.

Carol, behind Pippa, said, 'Oh, look at her! Teacher's pet!'

Pippa reddened. She walked away to the barre, trying to pretend she hadn't heard, but she had heard all right. She bent down to adjust the elastic on her ballet shoes.

'Never mind her,' said Vibeke, who was practising an exercise at the barre. 'She's just jealous.'

Vibeke was nice. She had a lot of wild dark hair, vivid brown eyes and warm brown skin. She was a few months older than Pippa, and had been in the class much longer. Vibeke had looked after Pippa when she joined the class. They had shared sweets and cartons of drinks. They had always stood next to one another, and partnered one another until recently, when Vibeke had shot up in height and been transferred to the front line of older, more experienced girls.

Pippa said, 'Why does she always pick on me? I

8

wasn't trying to show off, honest!'

'No, but you're heaps better than she is, even though you've only been with us for a short time. Little Miss Carol is afraid you'll steal her place.'

'What place?'

'In the pantomime, of course!'

'Oh, do we give a show at the end of term?'

'You *are* dumb, aren't you! I said pantomime, and I meant pantomime. In the Theatre Royal in town.'

Pippa blinked. She'd been to a pantomime at the big Theatre Royal in the town centre a couple of years ago with a school friend. It had been magic. She'd wanted to go again last winter, but her mum had said no, she was too busy, so they hadn't gone. Her school friend had moved away, so there hadn't been any other way she could go.

Just then Madame called out the names of the ten oldest girls to line up at the front. Vibeke was one of them, and Carol another.

Pippa returned to her usual place in the back line, and they went on with the session. Madame was teaching them a new dance sequence, and instead of using the barre, they practised in pairs. Pippa's partner was a nice little girl, a relative newcomer called Betty with long yellow curls and blue eyes. Betty found the new dance sequence hard, but she persevered until she got it right. She jumped up and down, pleased with herself.

'Yes, I know it is hard,' said Madame, as she dismissed the class for the day. 'But it is great fun to do. Vibeke my dear, what is the matter with your foot?'

'It was just a scrape, Madame. Truly, it hardly hurts at all.'

'You get that foot looked at by a doctor, tonight. Understood?'

'Yes, Madame.'

The class was over. Pippa took off her shoes and put them into her dancing bag. Most of the other girls came for jazz dance lessons on a Tuesday as well, but Pippa's mother was often too busy to bring her. Pippa tried not to think about it too much, because it was awful when she looked forward to the Tuesday lesson, and then couldn't go.

It might well be seven whole days before she could dance again.

Except for practising in her room, of course. Oh, if only she had a bit more space and a tape recorder, instead of having to borrow her brother's Walkman all the time!

Carol shoved past Pippa to reach her anorak. Pippa moved back to give Carol plenty of room, because Carol was the sort that dug her elbow into you if you didn't.

'There, you see! It didn't do you any good, sucking up to teacher, did it?'

'I wasn't,' said Pippa, trying to keep the peace.

'Yah, anyway!' said Carol, giving her a vicious look. 'You saw what happened? I'm in the front row, and we're the ones who'll get through the audition, and you lot at the back won't stand an earthly.'

Pippa would have liked to know more about the audition, but Carol was definitely not the right person to ask, and Vibeke was talking to the girl who had been her partner in the last exercise.

Pippa went out into the dark October night. Even the street lights seemed dim after the brightness of the studio. She probably wouldn't have another chance to talk to Vibeke until next week, because most of the girls in the dancing class, including Vibeke, went to the private school on the common. Pippa was at the local state school.

Pippa's mother was waiting outside in the car, working her way impatiently down the crossword in the paper.

'You're late!' she said, slamming the car into gear and driving off into the traffic before Pippa had fairly got her seat belt on.

'Sorry,' said Pippa. It wasn't worth arguing, although the clock on the dashboard said it was only five minutes after the time the class was supposed to finish.

'I don't suppose you've remembered,' said Mrs Fox, 'but it's Open Night at your brother's school. I've had to cancel a committee meeting so that we can get there . . . your father's working late . . . what does that driver think he's doing . . . ? Some people aren't fit to be let loose on the roads. We'll hardly have time to eat before we have to be off again. If you insist on having dancing lessons, why can't you go to the woman at the Methodist church?'

Pippa thought, Because she's no good. But she didn't say so. She didn't argue with her mum. Not many people did. Her mum was the sort who told you what to do, and you did it. Mrs Fox told people what to do all day long, up at the Technical College where she was Head of Administration. It was she who had found out that Madame was supposed to be the best dance teacher in town, and got Pippa enrolled.

Pippa thought, I must work on my left ankle. Vibeke's feet make a beautiful curve . . .

Mrs Fox said, 'Pippa! You're day-dreaming again. I said, you'll have to change into something decent before we go. We can't have you turning up for Open Day at Netley in your dancing clothes.'

11

'Yes, Mum. Mum, one of the girls in the dancing class said that there might be a chance of . . .'

'Will you look at that! The way she cut me up! What appalling driving! We'll just have to bolt down some food and get on over there. We mustn't be late. It's most important that we talk to the teachers at Tom's new school. He seems to be doing so well . . . worth it, though it does cost an arm and a leg each term . . .'

Still talking, Mrs Fox inched the car onto the hard standing area in front of their house.

Pippa helped her mother unload her coat and brief-case from the car, and followed her through the hall into the big kitchen at the back, where Tom was spooning a bought salad mix and oven chips onto plates of cold meat.

Tom was good-looking, in a dark, mischievous way. He was also brainy, with the sort of happy-go-lucky temperament which made everyone smile when he came into a room. He'd shot up recently, and his voice had broken. Sometimes when Pippa looked at him, she found it hard to recognise him as her brother.

Pippa was different. She was small with long straight fair hair, and she wasn't much good at anything except dancing, and that didn't count in this house.

'Five minutes, and we must be off,' said Mrs Fox.

'Plenty of time,' said Tom. 'How was the class, Pippa? Managed to get up on your pointes yet?'

Pippa grinned at him. 'Not yet, silly. We don't go on pointes till we're twelve, at least. But we did this new dance . . .'

'Go and change first,' said Mrs Fox. 'We mustn't be late for Tom's first Open Day.'

Tom said, 'Don't fuss, Mum. I expect it'll be just the same as at the old school. Queues of parents all worrying about whether their little darlings are going to get through their exams and come out with scholarships to Oxbridge . . .'

Mrs Fox smiled at him, and touched his shoulder. 'Well, of course, parents do hope, naturally . . .'

Pippa tore up the stairs with her dancing bag bumping along behind her. She slipped off her dancing clothes, pushed them into the linen basket on the landing to be washed, and pulled on a jumper and jeans. Then she remembered that her mother had told her not to wear jeans to go to Netley . . . 'We must make a good impression, not let Tom down . . .'

Pippa wriggled out of the jeans and pulled on a skirt that she thought was far too old for her, but that her mother liked. A quick brush of her straight fair hair, and an even quicker pass with a wet flannel, into her best black shoes, and she was off down the stairs again.

'Can't you find anything better to wear?' said her mum. 'Oh, well. No time to change again.'

Netley was a private school set in its own grounds. It had an agreeable air of having been there for a long time, and knowing more than you did about everything.

'Oh, Tom, I'd forgotten it was so nice!' said Mrs Fox, impressed.

'It's all right,' said Tom. 'You soon get used to it.'

Pippa was all eyes. They had a proper stage in the hall, with lights, and curtains, and backcloths. What a terrific place for a show, almost as good as the theatre in town! If Vibeke got into the pantomime this Christmas, then perhaps Pippa could persuade her parents to take her. Or, if they wouldn't take her, then perhaps she could go with one of the other girls from the dancing class. It would be really great to see Vibeke on the stage . . .

'Come along, Pippa. Well, Tom, that was a good report, wasn't it? Now where do we go . . . ?'

Pippa wondered which pantomime it would be. She'd seen Cinderella before. The fairy godmother had had a dance which Pippa had tried to copy at home . . .

'Pippa! Day-dreaming again! Come along, child!'

. . . she couldn't quite remember how it had gone, now. The fairy had worn the most beautiful lilac costume with silver sequins on it. She'd gone up on her pointes and . . .

'Of course we can manage Friday evenings!' Mrs Fox was saying. She was smiling, really over the moon about something.

Friday evenings? Pippa woke up. Fridays was her dance class. She looked at Tom, and he was grinning, too.

The master was smiling, too. 'It'll be hard work, remember, but Tom shows promise, and who knows, with extra practice . . . certainly the third eleven . . . possibly the second . . .'

Pippa tried to make sense of what was happening, but she'd been thinking about other things too hard. The clock on the wall told her they'd been at the school for nearly two hours.

Mrs Fox was shaking hands with the master, and they were leaving, walking back along the echoing corridors to the front door and the car park.

'What was that about Fridays?' said Pippa.

'Extra cricket practice,' said Tom, taking the front seat as of right while Pippa slid into the back. 'They think I might have a chance of making one of the cricket teams next summer, if I fit in some extra practice on Friday evenings. They use the indoor net in the sports hall.'

14

Mrs Fox said, 'I'm thrilled, Tom! Just thrilled! Only think! So soon! What does that driver think he's . . . ! And Fridays, it's really quite convenient. I can nearly always fetch you . . .'

Pippa said, in a small voice, 'Friday is my dancing class.'

'What?' Mrs Fox's voice sharpened. 'Oh. Yes, so it is. I'd forgotten, but . . . well, we'll have to see what we can do. We can't let this chance slip by for Tom, and it isn't as if you are ever going to break any records, is it? I know! If you're really so set on continuing, then you can go to the woman at the Methodist church in future!'

Pippa thought, I can't bear it! I'll die!

Chapter Two

Pippa was daydreaming. She imagined herself back in the dancing class. Madame was saying, 'The rest of you line up at the back, in pairs. Now I want you to watch very carefully. This is a new dance, called the polka. It isn't easy. The basic step goes like this . . .'

Madame demonstrated. And again. She showed the girls how to bring their left feet smartly up to the back of their calves at the end of the step. To make matters worse, they had to turn and turn, and turn again while doing this difficult step.

When Madame had demonstrated again, and again, the girls tried. Pippa could feel the music telling her what to do, but Betty was clumsy, and couldn't do it.

Most of the front line got it right. Vibeke and her partner did. Carol's partner was all over the place. Pippa could see that Carol was angry, because her partner was slow to learn the step. It made Pippa feel a bit better when Betty messed it up.

But Betty tried hard. She asked Pippa to show her how she did it, when they rested for a while. Pippa showed Betty, and Betty copied her, and very soon Betty was getting it right. Betty jumped up and down, pleased with herself . . .

'Pippa! You are not paying attention! What have I just

said you are to do for homework?'

Pippa jumped, and looked around her. She wasn't in the dancing class. Her mum had stopped her going to dancing classes. She was at school, and she'd missed everything the teacher had said.

Miss Masters was angry.

'Stand up, Pippa. You're been day-dreaming again. I don't suppose you have the slightest idea of what's been going on this lesson. Have you?'

Pippa laced her hands behind her back, and wondered how long it would be before the bell went for the end of the school day.

'No answer? I suppose that's answer enough. You will stay behind when the bell goes.'

Pippa sat down, feeling numb. She had suspected for some time that Miss Masters didn't like her. There was no mistaking that particular tone in a teacher's voice.

She hoped her mother would be late home that evening, and wouldn't know anything about it. Pippa had never been kept behind after school before. She wasn't brilliant like Tom, but she could usually manage to get by.

The bell went, and the rest of the class scrambled out and away. Miss Masters gestured for Pippa to approach her desk.

'What's the matter with you, Pippa? You don't seem quite with us nowadays.'

'Sorry, miss. Got a cold coming.' Pippa managed to cough. It was true, she did feel as if she had a cold coming.

'Hm. All right. I'll let you off just this once. But, Pippa, I've been wanting to speak to you for some time. I taught your brother, you know, and . . .'

Pippa looked at the floor. She knew the rest of it by

heart, because she'd been following Tom up the classes through the first, and now the middle school. Sooner or later the teachers all said how disappointed they were that Pippa wasn't more like her brother, and she could at least make an effort, couldn't she?

'Sorry, miss,' said Pippa, when the lecture was over.

After she'd left school Pippa realised she hadn't found out what the homework was, after all. Maybe she wouldn't go into school tomorrow. Maybe she'd really have a cold, and get her mum to write a note to excuse her. She was never going to be any good at school, so what did it matter if she went or not?

She walked home by herself. She'd had one best friend, but that family had moved away and none of the other girls seemed very interested in being friends with her. Pippa had hoped that a bubbly girl called Janet would be her friend, and for a couple of weeks Janet had walked home with her. But then Janet had been taken over by another girl in the class, and though she'd asked Pippa to her birthday party, Pippa hadn't been able to go. Janet hadn't been so friendly since.

That had been very unlucky. Pippa had wanted to go to the party but Tom had been playing in a cricket match. Her mum had wanted to go to the cricket match, and it wouldn't have been possible for her to get Pippa to the birthday party and back. So Pippa had had to refuse.

She'd tried to tell Janet how it was at home, but Janet hadn't understood.

Tom told Pippa that it was her own fault if she didn't make friends, but it wasn't that easy. Pippa did try to talk to other girls now and again, but she never seemed able to think of anything interesting to say.

She turned into their driveway and looked up at the dark red brick of the house, with its double-fronted bay windows, and heavy gabled porch.

She thought, I don't like this house.

It wasn't a new thought, but it was the first time she'd brought it out from the back of her mind and looked at it. She'd liked the house they'd had before, not so very far away, but much smaller and, well, more friendly in every way. This house felt cold, and her room was even smaller than the one she'd had before.

Tom had a brilliant big room all to himself on the first floor overlooking the road, where he could lay out his computers and his games and have his telly on in bed if he liked.

Pippa had the small bedroom at the back of the house. She tried to keep a space clear between the bed and the built-in cupboards to practise, but it meant putting her desk and chair on the bed while she did so. Everything had to be put away as soon as she used it, and that was difficult because her mother kept all the spare linen in the built-in cupboard in her room.

Only, now the dancing classes had stopped, Pippa didn't bother to keep her room tidy. She disliked living in a muddle, but she just didn't have the heart to tidy up.

It was ten days since Pippa had been to dancing class. She sat on her bed and looked at the floor between her feet. Her feet were half in and half out of her shoes, the toes pointing in.

She was still wearing her school uniform, although she was supposed to change out of it as soon as she got home from school. She'd managed to get three days off school with her 'cold' but today she'd gone back, and she wished she hadn't because now she was more behind than before.

Mrs Fox pushed the door open and dumped a pile of linen on the bed.

'This room is a tip! I don't know what's got into you, really I don't. You could have tidied it up while you were off with your cold. And why don't you want any supper?'

'I'm not hungry.'

'You've got to eat. "Feed a cold and starve a fever." Oh, by the way, that Madame of yours left a message on the Ansaphone. Says she's missed you, the last couple of lessons. I really must get round to writing to tell her you're not coming back. I paid her for the term in advance, so I don't know what she's griping about.'

Pippa felt a stir of interest. 'Madame always asks after people if they're ill. My friend Vibeke had a bad foot, and Madame noticed, straight away.'

'So she should. It's a pity you've had to leave, but there it is. I've rung up the other dancing class and they say they'll take you, even half way through the term.'

Pippa cringed. 'Honest, Mum, I can't go there. It's kids' stuff.'

'Nonsense, it's perfectly adequate.'

'But Mum, it's really for little ones up to the age of seven. They pretend to be trees and elves, and dance around toadstools. They have to be taught how to march in time to the music, and to skip, and sing nursery rhymes. It's not a proper dancing class.'

'Well, it sounds perfectly lovely to me, but if you want to cut off your nose to spite your face, I can't stop you. Luckily I haven't paid her yet, or that would be two lots of fees down the drain. But it's your choice, remember. If you don't want to go, fair enough, but I must insist that you behave yourself when you come downstairs. Anybody else would be pleased that their brother was doing so well.'

'I am,' said Pippa.

'You never think of anyone but yourself, that's your trouble,' said her mum. 'It's very self-centred of you. I won't say "selfish" though sometimes I think . . . but you do realise that everyone has to make sacrifices sometimes, don't you? Look at me. Rushed off my feet trying to do my job and run this house and see to you two kids. And your father. Look at the long hours he puts in. We wouldn't have two holidays abroad each year and run two cars and have this lovely big house if we didn't work so hard, not to mention paying Tom's fees at Netley. So let's have a smile, shall we?'

'I'm sorry,' said Pippa, holding back tears.

'Well . . .' Her mum put her hand on Pippa's shoulder, and pressed it. 'We'll have to see what we can do to make up to you. An outing or something. Right?'

'Right,' said Pippa, trying to smile. The smile lasted as long as Mrs Fox was in the room, but when she went, Pippa began to cry. Mrs Fox had left the pile of linen on the bed. Pippa pushed it off onto the floor, and lay down with her head under the pillow.

Pippa's dad opened the door into the darkened bedroom, and tiptoed in. Pippa wasn't asleep. She sat up in bed, and put on the bedside light. He smiled at her, and she smiled back. He put a Mars bar on the bed, and sat down. He was a big man, and his weight made the bed sag, but Pippa didn't care.

'Mind you clean your teeth afterwards.'

'Mm. Wow. I do like Mars. Thanks.'

'Worried about you, Mouse.' "Mouse" was his pet

name for her. 'You're looking peaky. Got to feed you up after that cold, eh?'

'I'm all right. Just not very hungry.'

'Missing your dancing lessons, I hear. Sorry about that. Bad luck. Tell you what: take you with me to the indoor tennis courts some time. Get you some coaching.'

'Thanks.'

'Don't sound so enthusiastic!'

'Sorry. I didn't mean . . . Thanks, that would be lovely. But, Dad?'

'Yes, Mouse?'

'This room's awfully small. I know Mum likes to keep the spare room all nice and neat for visitors, but you know the rooms in the loft that the people before us put in . . . couldn't I move up there? I know the bathroom's not finished, and there's no carpets or anything, but it wouldn't cost much to put some curtains up at the window and perhaps I could have that old carpet that Mum threw out when she got a new one and . . .'

'Whatever will you think of next? Don't be daft, love. There's no heating up there. You'd freeze to death. When we can afford it, some time next year, perhaps, we'll extend the central heating up there, and finish the bathroom, and then we'll see, shall we? Do you want a glass of milk?'

Pippa shook her head. He kissed her, turned off the light and went out. Pippa stared up into the dark. It would have been nice to have had a room with a bit of space in. Perhaps she could have kept up with her practice, then. Though what was the point? It was thirteen days since she'd been to a dancing class. She was in trouble at school. She'd had a whole row of Ds and Es lately. Well, she didn't care. She wasn't like Tom and the sooner they realised it, the better.

Tom banged on the door and barged in.

'Hey, Pippa! Wake up! It's me! Big brother! Hey, don't you ever put anything away in your room?'

He pushed some clothes off the chair and sat down on it, making it creak. 'Mum said if you really feel sick, you'd better go straight to bed, and I'm to call the doctor if you get worse. She's gone to a meeting.'

Pippa nodded, but didn't lift her head from her pillow. She was lying on the bed, still wearing her school uniform.

'Want to come down to watch telly?'

She shook her head.

'Want some food? I can microwave you something if you like.'

She said 'No, thanks, I'm all right,' in a soft voice.

Tom pulled a face. 'Look, I'm sorry you're feeling rotten, and I'm sorry about the dancing classes. But aren't you making a bit of a meal of it?'

'I'm trying not to, that's why I'm keeping out of the way. I am happy for you, really I am, Tom.'

Tom fidgeted and the chair creaked again.

'Well, the way you act, it's embarrassing. After all, you could have gone to the other class on Wednesday.'

'No, I couldn't.' Pippa sat up and wound her arms round her legs. 'Tom, there is something you could do for me. I promise I won't talk about the dancing class again, but do you think you could take me to the pantomime in the Theatre Royal at Christmas? My friend Vibeke may be in the pantomime, and I'd really like to see her.'

'Sure. No probs.'

Pippa said, 'I'm sorry if I was knacky. It's not your

fault. Did your cricket practice go all right tonight?'

'Yeah. Brill. I've got to keep practising, though.'

Pippa nodded. She knew all about that.

Tom got off the chair, which creaked again. He was having a glorious time in and out of school. It was nice of him to bother with her.

He said, 'You don't eat enough to keep a flea alive. Are you sure you don't want me to call the doctor?'

'I'll come down and get a sandwich.'

That made him feel better. He leapt down the stairs, three at a time, whistling a pop tune off key. She followed, slowly. On the landing there was a glass-fronted cabinet which contained their mother's collection of thimbles, and the sporting trophies which her father had won as a young man. He'd been a sprinter, and then he'd gone in for tennis seriously. Cups galore. Pretty things in plenty.

Pippa looked at the cabinet, and all the itty bitty pretty things, and she had a sudden urge to smash it in. To crash through the glass, and sweep everything in there to the floor, and then trample, and bash and crash . . .

'Pippa? Come on . . . !'

She took a big breath, and felt the house re-settle around her. That had been a near thing. She held onto the bannister as she went down the stairs. She was still feeling giddy when she got to the bottom.

She thought, I hate this house. I hate that cabinet. I hate my nasty little room. I hate . . . everything.

She thought, I ought to be ashamed of myself. But I'm not. I hate them. I almost hate Tom at times.

As she passed the big Victorian wardrobe in the hall, she saw her reflection in the wavering surface of its mirror. 'What a pale little thing you are!' she said to herself. 'You're almost not there at all.'

Chapter Three

Mrs Fox was always saying she never got through a meal without being interrupted by the phone. Tonight was no exception.

'Well!' she said, returning to her cooling meal. 'You'll never guess who that was!'

'I know!' said Mr Fox, smiling. 'Either a double glazing salesman, or someone offering us a holiday for two in Tenerife . . .'

'Silly!' She hit the top of his shoulder, and picked up her knife and fork. 'I don't know if it's good news or not. Surprising, anyway. Pippa, that was your Madame from the dancing class. Honestly, Tom, if you eat as fast as that, you'll choke!'

Pippa looked up. She'd been pushing her food about her plate.

Mrs Fox forked food into her mouth, elegant even in her haste. 'Wanted to know why you hadn't been for some weeks. I thought I'd dropped her a line about it.'

'There, you see, Pippa,' said Mr Fox. 'You've been missed.'

'Mm,' said Mrs Fox. 'Madame wants her back. I explained about Tom's extra coaching. She was quite shirty. A bit cheeky, I thought. I mean . . . Netley, and all that.'

Tom choked on his food, and his dad hit him on the back. 'Sorry,' he said, gulping water. 'Honest, Mum, extra cricket practice is not that important. I almost wish they hadn't said anything.'

'Nonsense, dear,' said his mum, in a sharp voice. 'Well, I told her, it would be very inconvenient, and I really didn't know how we'd manage, and it probably won't come to anything because the child hasn't been there for more than two ticks. But I did agree she could go, if she wanted to. I must need my head examining.'

Pippa looked puzzled, and her dad said, 'Let's take if from the beginning, shall we? What is it that Madame wants?'

'She wants Pippa to take part in an audition for a dancing show, end of term concert, perhaps? Something like that. It's on Tuesday next, instead of the usual jazz session. I said I'd ask the child if she wanted to go, and then we'd see. I tried to make it clear that there's no way we can get her there on Fridays, but Madame wouldn't let me get a word in edgeways. Kept going on and on about how she thought Pippa had what it takes . . . whatever she means by that!'

Pippa didn't know whether to be pleased or pretend it didn't matter if she went or not.

'End of term show?' said Tom. 'That'll be fun. We'll all come and watch you be a fairy dancing round a toadstool, shall we?'

'Oh, you!' said Pippa, but she smiled, all the same.

'No chance of that,' said Mrs Fox. 'I made it quite clear that this is a one off, next Tuesday evening only. Pippa, are your dancing things clean? I don't have time to do anything about it if they aren't.'

A wonderful thought came into the back of Pippa's mind, and grew and grew. Just suppose the audition was for the pantomime, and not for an end of term show? Vibeke had said there wasn't any end of term show. Carol had been jealous of Pippa because she'd thought Pippa might take her place in the pantomine chorus.

Could it be true? If so . . .

Pippa took a deep breath. She thought she'd burst if she didn't tell somebody. She helped Tom clear the table and stack everything in the dishwasher.

'Tom, there is no end of term concert. But Madame does hold auditions for the children's chorus in the pantomime at the Theatre Royal. I know I haven't been at the dancing class very long, but Madame did say I was doing all right. Do you think I might get in?'

'Oh, come on! It's hardly likely, is it!'

Pippa felt as if he'd doused her with cold water. No, of course it wasn't likely that anything that marvellous could happen to her.

'Take it from me, it's an end of term show. We have one at Netley, of course. I'm going to be in one of the sketches. Mum's got to make me a special costume. It's a secret, what I am, but maybe I'll tell you, nearer the time . . .'

Pippa thought that if he mentioned Netley just once more, she'd crown him with the saucepan.

'. . . and anyway,' said Tom, 'you can't go back to the dancing classes, so I really don't see much point in your going to the audition, do you?'

'No, I suppose not. But I am going, all the same.'

Of course Tom was right. She almost wished Madame hadn't asked for her. It was awful to look forward to something, and then have it cancelled.

She went upstairs and got out her dance things. They were clean. She went up on her toes and felt her muscles complain as she held the pose. She would have to put in some practice before Monday. Even if it was the last time she ever went, she didn't want to disgrace herself.

She cleared a space on the floor. Up, two three . . . arms, two three . . . turn, two three. . . .

. . . . bend back and to the left, right foot pointing . . . and up . . . and turn. It was coming back, slowly. She began to look forward to Tuesday.

Pippa couldn't keep her mind on school. She pushed everything out of her mind except the audition. She practised all weekend. She made an excuse not to go with her father when he wanted to take her down to the tennis club. She hadn't got a minute to waste.

She went up to the cold bright attic to practise her tap dancing, because otherwise her mother would hear her and complain about the noise. Pippa worked hard.

One of the trickiest things was the time step. It had to be neat and snappy, with a clear sharp sound from your feet. Pippa had always shuffled through it before, but now it was beginning to come . . .

That left ankle of hers . . . oh well. She had done her best.

She zoomed out of school on Tuesday and stood there, hopping from one foot to the other with her dance bag swinging from her arm. Her mum had arranged for a neighbour to collect Pippa and take her to the audition.

She waited and waited.

Quarter past. Half past.

The neighbour wasn't coming.

From feeling marvellous, Pippa felt so miserable she could hardly stand upright.

She pushed herself off the school gatepost, and started to walk home. She usually did walk home. It wasn't that far. But the audition was to be held in a Dance Studio some way beyond her house, and that was too far to walk. Pippa knew she'd never get there in time. She was going to miss her big chance.

Perp, perp! Someone was using their car horn beside her.

'Pippa! Do you want a lift?'

It was Vibeke, in the front seat of a spanking new little red car. Two smiling faces. One was Vibeke's, and the other was that of a stranger with short soft brown hair.

'Hop in!' cried Vibeke. 'Wait a mo! I'll get out, and you can get in the back with me. Oh, this is Marianne. She's our new au pair. She's nice.'

Pippa smiled at Marianne, who smiled back. Marianne had a gold filling on one of her upper teeth. She wore an enormous T-shirt and colourful baggy trousers. Pippa agreed with Vibeke. Marianne was nice.

Pippa climbed in beside Vibeke, who couldn't seem to stop talking.

'. . . I knew you were coming because Madame asked if I knew why you hadn't been lately, and of course I didn't, but I knew you'd be thrilled, so Madame said she'd ring up and explain it to your mum, and that's why I was looking out for you . . .'

Pippa threw herself back in the car, and smiled. She would have pinched herself, only it would hurt. She couldn't believe her good luck.

'. . . and I've been practising all weekend, haven't you, and Carol's been showing off, saying she'd just walk it, and so I reminded her that the audition is open to everyone, for people from all the other dancing classes in town, and oh, just anybody who fancies their chances, and that some of them will be really good, practically going to stage schools and I also told her you'd be coming, and you should have seen her face, honest, you'd have thought she'd swallowed a plum-stone . . .'

'Vibeke!' said Pippa.

'. . . and I reminded her that Madame said her arms were like dried twigs . . .'

'Vibeke!' said Marianne and Pippa together. Then they all burst out laughing.

'Sorry!' said Vibeke. 'I know I talk too much, but isn't it exciting!'

'Yes,' said Pippa. Excitement didn't make her want to talk. It made her glow from the inside. 'Vibeke, this audition is not for an end of term show, is it?'

'Course not. I told you. Madame doesn't have an end of term show in December because of the pantomime. Madame has a contract to train two teams of children's dancers for the Theatre Royal pantomime each year. There has to be two teams, because children only appear on stage every other night. And matinées, of course.

'I just missed a place last year, because I'd sprained my ankle and it really wasn't strong enough to dance on, but I was First Reserve and went to all the rehearsals and if anyone had dropped out, I'd have been on. Carol was in it, and almost all the older ones in the dancing class. I went to see them three times. It was magic.'

Pippa tried to remember how many children usually attended Madame's classes. About thirty, she thought, and most of them had been at the dancing class longer than Pippa. And Vibeke had said there would be lots of children coming in from outside. Yet Madame had made a special point of ensuring that Pippa attended the audition. Could it be possible that Madame would select her, Pippa . . . and if so, what would her mother say?

She wouldn't think about that, now. She would put all thoughts of the pantomime out of her head, and just enjoy what she'd got. One hour and a half of dancing! Magic!

She floated rather than walked into the audition. It was being held in a proper dance studio, instead of the hall in which they normally practised. There were barres round three sides of the room, and mirrors on the fourth wall.

There was a battered-looking piano, and a woman to play the music, instead of the usual tape recorder. And hordes of excited children and mothers. Everyone was so excited that they either all talked at once, or stood silent, looking nervous.

Pippa saw Madame's royal blue strip everywhere, but there were a lot of other children there, wearing all the colours of the rainbow. Pippa shrank against the wall.

'Ah, there you are!' said Madame, and gave Pippa a special light touch on her forehead which was better than a kiss. 'Hurry up and change into your ballet shoes. Marianne dear, you will wait outside with the mothers, won't you? All the mothers to wait next door, please!'

Marianne blew them a kiss and departed, and so did all the mothers.

'Now remember,' Vibeke said to Pippa as they changed, 'smile! You've got to look as if you're having a wonderful time!'

Pippa nodded. That wouldn't be difficult. Once her dancing shoes were on, she was a different person. And the way she felt now, it would take a lot to stop her smiling.

'Now girls,' said Madame. 'Into four lines. The tallest ones at the front. Spread out. I know you're all very excited, but we'll get straight down to it, shall we. . . . ?'

Chapter Four

The lesson began. Only it wasn't like any other lesson. Madame taught them a sequence of steps, linking them together to form a short dance. Most of the steps they'd done before in class, and they were not difficult in themselves.

'But remember your head positions, and smile!' said Madame.

The difficult thing was to remember the order in which the steps came. The girl on Pippa's left kept muttering the sequence to herself, and hesitating. Pippa didn't think it was that hard. She learned quickly, when she put her mind to it.

Then Madame gave them an audition. She started with the front line of older girls. They had to come to the front in groups of four and perform to music the dance she had just taught them, while the others looked on and waited for their turn.

Madame made notes as they went along, which was unnerving.

Pippa felt she was lucky not to have been in the front line, because it gave her extra time to watch and remember the sequence of steps.

Then it was her turn. The music started. Pippa went up on her toes. Her feet obeyed her, even that awkward left ankle was almost coming into the right position. She smiled and smiled, because it was so wonderful to be dancing again.

When it was over, she went to sit at the side with Vibeke, who nodded and held up her thumb to show that she thought Pippa had done all right. The girl on Pippa's left was biting her lip and tossing her hair back. She hadn't done so well, Pippa knew.

'. . . and the last group,' said Madame. 'Splendid. Most of you have been very quick to learn, and that's one of the things I'm looking for. Now I'm going to ask you to sing.' There was a rustle of dismay, and Madame smiled. 'Come on, it's a song you all know, because we did it last term in our show. "The sun has got his hat on . . ." You all know that, don't you? Right! Come to the front and sing it for me in the same groups of four as before. Wait for the music and off you go.'

The first four girls sang with verve, and two of them even managed a smile all through. To Pippa's ear, one of them sang slightly flat. Madame seemed to think so, too, because she listened very closely before she went on to Carol's group.

You could hear Carol's voice coming through strong and sure, leading the others. Carol managed to smile, too. Madame smiled and nodded, and gestured the next four to come on.

This time Pippa was pretty sure that one of the girls wasn't singing at all, because only a tiny sound came from the group. Everyone laughed, but Madame frowned, and made them try again. This time they sang more loudly, but Pippa, watching, thought it possible that one of the girls was just miming.

'Hm-mm,' said Madame, and went on down the line. When it came to Pippa's four, the girl on the end burst into tears, and was going to run from the room, only Madame stopped her.

'Come along, my dear. The singing's not that important, because you'll never be asked to sing all on your own. No, never, I promise you. Go and blow your nose, and we'll put you into the next four . . . Betty, come and make up this four, will you, dear?'

Betty was the girl with long blonde curls and blue eyes who had been Pippa's partner in the polka. She looked like a little doll. She had a pretty, high but breathy voice. Pippa sang out as well as she could, but the other two didn't make much noise.

'Fine,' said Madame, when they had all finished. 'Now change into your tap shoes.'

Vibeke and Pippa met up where they'd left their things, and sat on the floor to change as quickly as they could.

'Phew!' said Vibeke, pushing tendrils of hair back off her forehead. 'It's not that it's so difficult, it's knowing that everyone's watching you, and waiting for you to make a slip so that they can get your place.'

'I'm sure you'll get in,' said Pippa. 'I've asked my brother to take me, so that I can see you.'

'Come off it!' said Vibeke. 'You'll be in it yourself, the way things are going!'

Carol stamped past them, and accidentally on purpose trod on the side of Pippa's leg.

'Ouch!' said Pippa.

'No need to make a fuss,' said Carol. 'I just didn't see you.'

Vibeke said, 'Of course you saw her! You . . .'

'I said I didn't see her, and I didn't!' said Carol, and marched on with her nose in the air, making a great clatter with her tap shoes.

'Are you all right? Is it bleeding?' asked Vibeke.

'No,' said Pippa, breathing lightly because of the pain. 'It's just a graze.'

'Shall I tell Madame?'

'Oh, no. She might tell me to sit out for the rest of the audition. I'll be all right!'

'Up you get,' said Madame. 'Back into your lines. Now we will learn another sequence of steps, and I shall see how well you can remember and perform them. First we have a time step, three times, followed by . . . and . . . like this . . .'

Time step times three, said Pippa to herself, then four fast shuffles, then three scissors . . . no, there's something in between . . .

She counted on her fingers as Carol and Co. went through the routine. They did it well, with their heads up, and bright smiles on their faces.

'. . . and Vibeke and Co!' said Madame. Vibeke and her group swept off in great style, looking as if they were enjoying it, too. And the next group.

'. . . now you, Pippa!'

Pippa jumped. She'd thought Madame would start from the other end of the line as before, and she wasn't sure she was ready. But she lined up with the others, and went into the first of the time steps. Times three, thought Pippa. And now what? For one dreadful moment she couldn't remember what came next. And then she did, and swung into it as if she'd never had any doubts at all. The girl on her left wasn't too happy. She was biting her lip, and faltering, watching Pippa for a lead.

Pippa suddenly realised that she was very tense, and had forgotten to keep her head up and smile. Her leg was hurting, but she wasn't going to take any notice of that now. She lifted her head, and smiled at Madame. Her feet snapped along the floor, and her jumps were neat and clean when it came to the scissors.

'. . . and the next!' cried Madame, giving Pippa and her friends a nod of encouragement. But two of the next group had to struggle to get through, and one just gave up and stood still.

The next group didn't manage too badly, though their feet didn't make the right sort of crisp sound on the boards. Little Betty with the lovely long blonde curls was the only one who held up her head and smiled throughout, though her feet were sometimes a bit sloppy.

'Now take a rest, girls,' said Madame.

'Phew!' said Vibeke, collapsing next to Pippa. 'Listen, you did well! Carol was practically having kittens, while she was watching you.'

'I don't see why,' said Pippa, rubbing round the sore place on her leg. 'She's marvellous, and so are you. You're all bound to get in. As for me, well, I don't think Mum would let me, even if I did get in.'

'You're in, all right,' said Vibeke, wriggling her toes free of the tap shoes. 'Look at the way Madame smiled at you after you'd finished.'

Pippa thought how marvellous it would be to be grown up and in a pantomime. She would be wearing a beautiful tutu with sequins all over the bodice, and her hair swept up into a bun and crowned with a tiny gilded coronet. She would float across the stage on her pointes, and hold an arabesque until the audience gasped. She would look sad and mysterious, because . . . because she'd been magicked into a swan. Yes, that was right. She was a swan princess. The music would play low and sweet, and she would pirouette, and throw off a brilliant series of jetés.

Pippa could feel the warmth of the stage lights on her bare arms, and her legs quivered as if she were really dancing . . .

'Right, girls,' said Madame.

Vibeke nudged Pippa out of her daydream. Madame had some papers in her hand, and was leafing through them.

She was about to tell them who had been chosen for the pantomime. Pippa swallowed. Her hands felt sweaty. Would she be chosen? Oh, she must! She simply must! She'd die if she wasn't chosen!

'Now,' said Madame, 'you all know what this is about. I have to provide the Babes dancing chorus for the pantomime at the Theatre Royal this year. It's going to be Dick Whittington, and they've been lucky enough to get Nita Yorke as principal boy, and that nice man from the Saturday children's television programme to play King Rat.

'I have picked two teams of ten children each, with two understudies in case of accidents. Some of the children are from my dancing school, and some are not. The two teams will learn the dances and songs together, but will be appearing on alternate nights at the theatre. Some of you have done this before, and know what is involved. If you haven't been chosen before, then I will ring your parents to discuss the matter.

'The children I have chosen will be expected to report at the theatre three times a week, on Mondays, Wednesdays and Fridays, for the next four weeks. We may not always be able to get into the theatre itself, in which case we will rehearse in the hall nearby. There will be a great many routines to learn, and if anyone doesn't feel they are up to the work, or finds it too difficult, there will be no disgrace in their dropping out, and perhaps trying again another year.

'The two teams are as follows: A Team . . .' Madame read out the names of ten girls, who included six of the oldest from her class, and four from outside.

'And for the B team, 'Carol, Nicola, Tracy, Kate, Vibeke . . .' Carol grinned, and hugged herself, and the others looked pleased.

'. . . and the last one will be . . .' she paused and consulted her notes, 'the last one will be Betty.'

Pippa had been holding her breath, hoping against hope that her name would be the last one on the list. Betty gave a little hop of excitement, her blonde curls bouncing around her.

Pippa thought, But I was better than her!

'And,' said Madame, smiling at Pippa, 'I am appointing Pippa and Karina as First and Second Reserves!'

Chapter Five

Pippa changed back into her school clothes and stood hesitating by the door. Would Marianne give her a lift home? And what were her parents going to say when they heard what had happened?

Marianne came in, twirling her car keys. 'Is Vibeke ready?'

'Yes, I'm ready, I'm ready!' said Vibeke, jumping up to give Marianne a hug, and then giving Pippa a hug, too. 'I got in!'

'Of course you did,' said Marianne. 'And Pippa, too?'

'No,' said Pippa.

'Yes, you did. First Reserve. Someone's bound to drop out, and then you'll be in!'

Pippa watched as Betty dragged her mother over to Madame, and they began to talk. Betty hadn't been as good as Pippa. So why . . . ?

'Pippa, do you wish a lift in the car?' asked Marianne.

'Yes, of course she does! Come on, Pippa! Don't look so tragic. Oh, I forgot. Is your leg all right? Marianne, that horrid Carol trod on Pippa really hard, and then pretended she hadn't seen her!'

'Is all right?' Marianne asked Pippa. 'Let me look.'

'No, don't bother. It hardly hurts at all now,' said Pippa. She looked back at the room. It wasn't likely she'd see it again. She'd hoped for a while that her luck had changed, but it hadn't. Her mum had said No More Lessons, and no more lessons it would be.

'Pippa! A word!' It was Madame, hurrying over. 'My dear, has your mother called for you?'

'No, she couldn't get off work.' It was easier to lie than admit that her mother didn't care.

'I've phoned her several times, but she hasn't rung me back. Will you tell her that I'll try to call round this evening to have a word with her?'

'There you are,' said Vibeke. 'Madame will fix it. Oh, I just can't wait to start rehearsals. I wonder what sort of costumes we'll have in Dick Whittington.'

'What is this Dick Vittington?' asked Marianne.

Vibeke shrugged. 'Dunno. They didn't say.'

'There's a nursery rhyme with Dick Whittington in it,' said Pippa. ' "Turn again, turn again, Dick Whittington, Lord Mayor of London." I think there's a cat in it, too, but I can't remember why.'

'Who is this Maire?' said Marianne. 'Is it like the French Monsieur le Maire? Like the head of the town?'

''Specks so,' said Vibeke. 'Phew, am I flaked!' She lay back in the seat, and closed her eyes. Pippa looked at her anxiously. It did seem to her that Vibeke got tired awfully easily. She herself was tired, but not exhausted.

Marianne stopped in front of Pippa's house. It was only just around the corner from Vibeke's, yet they hadn't known they lived so close. That was because they went to different schools. Pippa got out and thanked Marianne for the lift. Vibeke opened her eyes and smiled, and then closed her eyes again. Pippa went indoors.

There wasn't anyone around to talk to. Tom had got his head down in his homework, and Mum wasn't back yet. Dad would be late, probably. There was a note on the kitchen table telling Pippa what to do about starting the supper, so that's what she did.

'I wonder what Dick Whittington is about,' thought Pippa. She wished . . . but it was no good wishing.

And yet perhaps it did do some good, after all. For that evening, while they were clearing away the supper things, Madame arrived and was taken into the front room by Mrs Fox.

'Who's the old bag, and what does she want?' asked Tom.

'She's Madame from the dancing school.'

'Oh. About that end of term show, I suppose. A pity you can't do it, really. It's great fun, being in a show. You can hear my lines, if you like. I've got the second biggest part in the sketch. You see, what happens is this . . .'

Pippa nodded in all the right places. He hadn't asked how she'd got on in the audition, although he expected her to listen while he told her everything he was doing in his show. Vibeke said boys were like that, and you couldn't expect anything else. Pippa didn't know much about boys. They were there at school, of course, but they didn't speak to her, and she certainly didn't speak to them.

She went into the hall and hovered outside the door of the front room. She could hear the murmur of voices, but there weren't any fireworks. She reckoned it would take her mother less than five minutes to say No, and see the visitor out.

Ten minutes passed. Pippa sat on the bottom-most stair, her eyes fixed on the door of the front room. A quarter of an hour. It was nearly twenty-five minutes before the door opened and they came out. Madame smiled at Pippa but didn't speak to her. Mrs Fox closed the front door behind her visitor, and stood there, adjusting one of her earrings.

Pippa hardly dared breathe.

Mrs Fox looked down at her. 'Well . . .' she said. She sounded unsure of herself for a change.

'Can I do it, then?' asked Pippa, beginning to hope.

'I don't know. As Madame says, it would be very good for you in many ways. I was most surprised when . . . but she says you learn quickly, and have a nice bright personality on the stage. I had no idea that . . . but . . . I still don't know how I could get you there and back.'

'I could take the bus.'

'You could get the bus there, perhaps, but . . . I couldn't let you do the journey back at night. And three times a week at least, and some weekends? What about your schoolwork? And there's no guarantee you'd ever go on stage, just being understudy. Madame said she would definitely have given you a place if you hadn't dropped out of her class without giving her any notice, and then it appears there's this other little girl whose elder sister always used to do it, and she learns very quickly indeed and her parents are very keen . . .'

'Betty,' said Pippa. So that explained why Betty had got the place. It just wasn't fair!

'I really don't know what to say. I told Madame I'd think it over, and I will ask your father when he comes in, of course, but I really don't think it's at all practical. There's your schoolwork, too. We don't want that to suffer. No, I think that on the whole it would be better if you put it out of your mind. Now be a good girl and don't sulk. I hate girls who sulk.'

'I'm not sulking,' said poor Pippa. After all, she hadn't

43

really expected it to work out, had she?

The phone rang. Mrs Fox answered it while Pippa went slowly up the stairs. It was all over, and she'd better forget about it. At least Tom had promised to take her to see the others dancing.

'Pippa! Come down! It's Mrs Cardoza, your friend Vibeke's mother, on the phone. I've often seen her at the Townswomen's Guild, but I didn't realise her daughter was in the Dancing Class, too. She says they have an au pair who is going to ferry Vibeke to and from the pantomime, and that she'd be happy to take you as well. How do you feel about that?'.

Pippa couldn't believe it. One minute everything was terrible, and the next, everything turned out all right!

'You mean I can do it?'

'Don't get so excited; you're only an understudy, remember.'

'Oh, Mum!' Pippa rushed down the stairs and hugged her mum around the waist. Mrs Fox laughed, and gave Pippa a brief hug before turning back to the phone. 'Yes, she'd love to. Of course I'll come to some arrangement with you about the petrol and . . .'

Pippa banged into Tom's room and said, 'I'm going to be in the panto! Or rather, First Reserve!'

'How come? I thought Fridays were out! You don't mean Mum has changed her mind . . .'

'No, silly. Your cricket practice is quite safe. My friend Vibeke's family has a nice au pair, and she's going to take us both and look after us. Isn't it fantastic?'

'Great,' said Tom. 'Now all we have to do is cross our fingers and hope someone breaks a leg so that you can go on at least once!'

'You mean thing! Of course I don't want anyone to break a leg . . .' though it did cross her mind that it wouldn't be a tragedy if something happened to Carol.

'So will you hear my lines, now?' said Tom.

'OK, but then I'm going to practise. Don't worry, I won't disturb you. I'll do it in the attic.'

'But it's freezing up there!'

'I don't care! I'm going to dance, and dance all night!' Pippa whirled round and round and round. Tom laughed, and threw his books into the air.

Mrs Fox was going bananas. One of her colleagues was off sick, and there was some kind of review due at work. Now Madame had given her a long list of things that needed to be bought, and a request for a licence to be obtained from the Town Hall, if you please!

'I'm not killing myself doing all this, until we know that you're definitely going on stage,' said Mrs Fox.

'But Mum, I'm going to need . . .'

'Just go off to rehearsal like a good girl, and let me be the judge of whether I should or should not spend all this money on you. Right?'

Pippa sighed. Vibeke had just been on the phone, trying to put Pippa in the picture about what was expected of the Babes. Pippa was in such a muddle about it she didn't know whether she hoped she would be able to go on stage, or not.

Marianne and Vibeke picked her up from school. Vibeke was trying to do her maths homework in the back.

'I had to promise my father I'd keep up with my schoolwork, whatever happened. How about you? Have you done your homework?'

Pippa grimaced. School was a bad word, nowadays.

'Marianne will help you, if you get stuck. Won't you, Marianne?'

'I will try. Pippa, how is your poor leg?'

'Better, thanks.'

The theatre was an old one near the city centre, at the back of the big shopping street. It was built of red brick, with pinnacles and minarets stuck all over the roof at the front. Across the building was an illuminated panel showing what play was running at the moment, and at the side were large posters advertising future events.

'Look!' screamed Vibeke, hopping around and pointing.

A yellow and red poster said, 'Dick Whittington' in large letters. Underneath were the names of Nita Yorke and Tony French, the nice man from children's television. There were other names, too, which the girls did not recognise, and half way down in small letters, 'Madame Tate's Babes'.

'That's us!' said Vibeke, 'Come on! This way!' She tore round the side of the theatre, and pounded up a narrow alley which seemed to be filled with large pieces of scenery. 'This is the Stage Door,' said Vibeke. 'This is where we go in. Bye, Marianne. See you later.'

'Wait, Vibeke!' said Marianne.

'And where do you think you're going?' said a large man in sweat-shirt and jogging trousers.

'Please, we're two of the Babes.'

'Can't you read?' He pointed to a chalked up notice at the side. 'Babes rehearsal in the hall opposite.'

'Oh, sorry,' said Vibeke, and set off in the opposite direction, dived across the main road outside, and disappeared up the steps of a new-looking hall.

'Vibeke!' cried Marianne, holding onto Pippa as if she might lose her, too.

Inside the building they went. A pianist was pounding out a well-known song, and there was Madame with the rest of the chosen girls. At Madame's side was a stranger, a man, with a smooth face and a receding hairline. His body was so graceful he didn't seem to have any bones in him. Except that he must have, or he'd fall down, thought Pippa.

Pippa didn't know whether to change into her dancing gear or not, but everyone else was doing so, so she did, too. Would she be needed or not? She didn't like to interrupt Madame's conversation with the man, to ask. Pippa thought she could work it out for herself. If all the girls from both teams were there, plus the other understudy, then she, Pippa, would not be needed. But every time she tried to count she got a different number of children.

Madame clapped her hands. 'Now I want you to line up in two rows, Team A across the front, and Team B across the back. Smallest children in the centre, moving outwards to the tallest at the sides.

'Yes, Betty, you are the smallest in Team B. Pippa, dear, where are you? Oh there you are. We've lost someone from Team A – skiing holiday – so I'm moving Kate up to Team A, and you'll take her place in Team B. Stand next to Betty in the middle. Now I'm going to give you all numbers, and you'll respond to numbers and not names in future. The smallest girls, that's Anna in Team A and Betty in Team B, are both number 1. The next smallest, that's Kate in Team A and Pippa in Team B, are both number 2 . . .'

Pippa said to herself, 'I'm number 2 . . . I must remember that!

'Now,' said Madame, 'You will often divide into two groups of five to make your entrances and exits. On those occasions you will be led on or off by your numbers 1 and 2, or by the tallest, who are numbers 9 and 10.

47

Carol was number 10 in the B team, and Vibeke was number 9. So Carol would always be on Pippa's side, but luckily, at the other end of the line, so they wouldn't have so much to do with one another.

'The uneven numbers will always lead on from Stage Right,' said Madame, 'which means that the even numbers will always lead on from Stage Left . . .'

Pippa was thrilled. Her dreams were going to come true, and she was actually going to be allowed to dance on a stage!

'Number 2, B team, which side do you come on?'

Pippa jerked to attention, 'Stage Left, Madame.'

'That's right. Now remember, there's no time for daydreaming here. There's plenty of other children wanting to take your place if you can't keep up.'

Pippa went red. She could see Carol giggling.

'Sorry, Madame.'

'Right. We'll start again. Put your hand up when I call out your numbers. One, two, three. . . . Fine. Now over to you, Ralph!'

Ralph was the boneless not-so-young man, and it appeared he was going to teach them their dances.

'We'll start with the opening number. You'll all be villagers with ballet shoes and full skirts. Even numbers enter Stage Left, odd numbers Stage Right. Numbers one and two lead on, with a skipping step to the count of eight, then one and two join hands and swing each other in the centre. . . . four and six join . . . eight and ten . . . and the same on the other side, for another count of eight. Have you got that? Yes? Good, let's try it. Off to the sides, numbers 1 and 2 ready to lead on. . . . Wait for the music and . . . off we go. . . . !'

Pippa grinned across the width of the stage area at Betty, who grinned back. They waited for the music, and skipped on to a count of eight. That took them into the centre of the stage area. They joined hands and swung in the centre, for another count of eight.

'Fine!' said Ralph. 'Now form two large circles, odd numbers Stage Left, even numbers Stage Right. Skipping steps, to the left, for a count of sixteen. Then back again, to your right. Nice and neat with your feet. Remember that; nice and neat with your feet. Wait for the music, and . . . off we go!'

Magic, thought Pippa. This is just plain magic.

But no more day-dreaming, or I'll be thrown out!

Chapter Six

'Pippa! Pippa Fox!'

Pippa scrambled her thoughts together and looked up at Miss Masters. She'd been day-dreaming again.

'Oh, Pippa,' said Miss Masters, and sighed. Everyone else in the class laughed, but Pippa went scarlet.

'Sorry, Miss Masters.'

'Come and see me at break time.'

Pippa looked at the questions on the board. Everyone else had been writing down answers in their rough books, but her book was blank, except for a drawing of a cat.

Hastily Pippa tried to remember what Miss Masters had been talking about, but she couldn't remember. She looked at the board, and couldn't think what the questions meant.

She panicked. She knew she spent too much time day-dreaming, but now she had something good to think about, and the rehearsals were hard and long, and she needed to keep going over the sequence of steps in her mind, and it just wasn't easy . . .

The bell went for break. Miss Masters motioned Pippa to stand by her desk.

'Well, Pippa? What do you have to say for yourself this time? Nothing? You're not going down with another cold? No? I would like to hear your explanation if you have one.'

Pippa remained silent, with her eyes on the floor.

'I think I've been very lenient with you up till now,' said Miss Masters, 'but kindness doesn't seem to have any effect. So you'll do one hour's detention after school.'

Pippa jumped. 'Oh no, Miss Masters! Not that! I can't! It would make me late!'

'You should have thought of that before.'

'But you don't understand!'

'Pippa, I have been trying to understand what makes you tick ever since you came into my class. I've tried to make allowances for you. I know you're not as clever as your brother, but until recently you did seem to be making some attempt to keep up with the rest of the class. But this last couple of weeks . . .'

'Please, please! Don't give me detention! I'll do extra homework, I promise! You see, I'm only in the B team because someone's dropped out, and if I don't get to the rehearsal they might give my place to someone else!'

'Slow down and try to tell me exactly what's going on.'

So Pippa told her, the words rushing out, and sometimes getting mixed up. She started in the middle and then had to go back to explain about only being First Reserve, and how there were rehearsals three nights a week and sometimes at weekends, too, and how Marianne and Vibeke picked her up outside school and took her to Vibeke's house where they had tea and did their homework before going off to rehearsal.

'. . . only Vibeke's at the private school and so is Carol and oh, most of the others, and their teacher under-

51

stands about the rehearsals and though they do have to work hard to keep up, she helps them. And . . . well, I know I'm a bit behind . . .'

There was a long silence. Pippa didn't dare look up, but it did seem to her that Miss Masters wasn't as angry as she had been.

'Vibeke?' said Miss Masters. 'And . . . Marianne, was it? Vibeke Cardoza? And Marianne is their new au pair?'

'Yes.' Pippa managed to look up, to find that Miss Masters wasn't looking angry at all.

'I know them. They go to my church. Why didn't you tell me about getting into the pantomime?'

Pippa hung her head again. 'I didn't think anyone would be interested.'

'You thought you might be teased, if everyone knew? I don't think you would, you know. But have it your own way. Now, we shall have to see what we can do to help you. There's no denying that you have fallen behind in class, and in theory it's not a good idea for anyone to take on extra work in the evenings when they are not coping too well at school. How do your parents feel about it?'

'They didn't ask how I was doing at school, so I didn't tell them about getting bad marks. You won't say, will you? They'd stop me dancing.'

'Hm. Do you think we could strike a bargain, you and I? You do your best to keep up at school, and I'll see what can be done to help you . . . then perhaps your parents need never know that you got so far behind.'

'Oh, thank you, Miss Masters. I will try, I promise!'

'Don't let me down, then. Now about tonight's home-work. I don't think you took in a word I said during the lesson. You'll have to read it up in this book . . . here, I'll lend you this copy . . . and then do the questions at the end of the chapter. Understood?'

'Oh yes! Thank you! Thank you!'

'Leave your thanks till we've seen whether you can cope or not. Now off you go to play. And, Pippa, let me know when you're going to be on stage, and I'll come and see you.'

By the end of the week, Pippa was mentally and physically worn out, and she knew that there was going to be a long rehearsal on Sunday.

She tried not to let her parents see that she was so tired, in case they withdrew her from the pantomime, but it was hard going. She had to be bright and cheerful all the time, and listen to Tom going on about Netley, and her mum going on about how much she had to do.

No one asked *her* how she was getting on. Well, Tom did once, and she was glad about that, but she could tell he wasn't really listening to what she said in reply. So she kept it short and said it was OK.

The worst thing was keeping to her bargain with Miss Masters. She dared not be caught daydreaming again. She had to listen and remember, and try to keep up with the others when all she wanted to do was put her head down on her desk and go to sleep.

At night she ate as much as she could, because she knew that if she didn't, she'd go all floppy. Then she had to do her homework, and find time to practise some of the awkward steps. Sometimes she and Vibeke could do their homework together and Marianne would help them, but not always. She wished she could ask Tom to help her, but the one time she hinted about it, he said she didn't know what homework was, and wait till she had to do two hours a night, like him!

So she did her homework as neatly as she could, and

forgot about watching even her favourite programmes on the telly. On Saturday evening she fell asleep as soon as she'd eaten her supper and gone up to her room. She didn't wake till the next morning, when she found she'd burrowed, fully dressed, into the bed-clothes! With her shoes on, even!

She still felt sleepy, but somehow she got ready and was waiting in the hall for Marianne and Vibeke when they came for her. Mr and Mrs Fox were taking Tom out for the day to a computer exhibition, so it had been arranged that Marianne would collect Pippa and give her lunch before they went off to the rehearsal.

'Wow, am I bushed! I'm so tired, I'm sleep-walking. And I've only just got up!' said Vibeke as Pippa climbed into the car.

'Me, too,' said Pippa. 'Where are we going?' because they were not going round the corner to Vibeke's house.

'Church, first. Then lunch back at our place. Then on to the theatre.'

Pippa shut her mouth and leaned back in her seat. The Fox family went to church at Christmas and Easter times, and of course they had Harvest and Carol services at school, but today wasn't that sort of special day, was it?

Pippa thought she'd better not say anything, or she'd never get to the rehearsal.

'Don't look so shattered,' said Vibeke, with another giant yawn. 'We don't have to stay in church with the grown-ups. It's stories and colouring for the younger ones, and drama and Yak-Yak for us.'

'Yak-Yak?'

'Talkshop. Jawshop, I call it. The teacher yaks on about something . . .'

Marianne said, 'Vibeke . . . that is not nice.'

'Well, she does go on a bit. Then we have to say what we'd do in the same circs, and why. Then she asks us if we can remember what Jesus did or said about it. Usually that's quite easy, but not always. Then games, sometimes. You know.'

Pippa didn't, but she didn't like to say so.

'Where do you go to church, Pippa?' said Marianne.

'The church on the High Street, sometimes. Not often, though.'

Vibeke said, 'Marianne says our church is not a bit like hers at home. They have lots and lots of statues in her church where she comes from, and pictures, and candles and incense. She gets homesick, you know.'

Pippa blushed for Vibeke. How could she talk like that in front of Marianne?

'Oh, you silly Vibeke!' said Marianne. 'Of course I miss my family, so many of us all living in one big house. But I like it here, too. And I would like you a lot better if you didn't talk so much, and listened to me for a change!'

Pippa waited for Vibeke to look upset, but Vibeke just leaned forward and hugged Marianne.

'Vibeke, wait till I park the car! Do you want to kill us all?'

Vibeke just laughed. Marianne parked the car in a tree-lined street, and they all got out.

Marianne said to Pippa, 'Do not mind Vibeke. She is a tease, no? I like my church at home, yes, but this one is nice, too. There are many young people, and we have much fun together. We have our own meetings on Sunday evenings, but tonight I must tell them I cannot come, for I think we will be at the theatre till late.'

'Come on, Pippa!' called Vibeke, disappearing into

the church. Pippa followed her into a bare, bright church. Several smiling grown-ups said hello to her.

Then Mr and Mrs Cardoza, Vibeke's parents, arrived with the two younger children. Mr Cardoza was a heart specialist, with a skin so dark it looked polished. Vibeke had explained to Pippa that her father wasn't called Dr, because although he was a doctor, he had been promoted to being a consultant, and now he was called Mr again. It was all very odd, but Pippa liked him because he treated her as if she were quite grown up, and listened to what she had to say, as if it really mattered.

Mrs Cardoza was nice, too. She laughed a lot and Pippa could see where Vibeke got her high spirits from. Mrs Cardoza had a creamy skin, and the children were all somewhere in between their father and their mother in looks and temperament.

'One, two, three, and Pippa makes four!' said Mr Cardoza, counting over the number of children in his party. 'All present and correct! So let's go in, shall we?'

Vibeke showed Pippa where they were to sit, and helped her find the first hymn. They had a short prayer, and then the children went out into a small hall at the side, and divided into age groups.

'Miss Masters!' said Pippa.

'I wondered if you'd turn up here today,' said Miss Masters, with a smile. She was to take their class!

There were about a dozen of them, all sitting around a couple of big tables. Miss Masters told them a true story, about three sisters. One was good at music and used to teach children how to play the piano. She used to play for ballet classes, and at church and whenever people wanted a singsong. The next sister was good at handling money, and she not only had a job in accounts but would help other people who were not so clever with their money. The third sister was a brilliant artist, but she never liked what she painted, and used to destroy it as soon as it was finished. People knew she was artistic, and would often ask her to do some work for them, but she always refused.

'Now,' said Miss Master, 'two of these people were always happy people and one was not. Can you tell me which one was always miserable?'

Vibeke's hand shot up. 'The one who wouldn't help others?'

'Yes, that's right. The poor soul couldn't think about anything but herself and that's a fine recipe for unhappiness, isn't it? Also, God gave her a very special gift or talent, and she didn't do anything with it, for herself or for other people. Now, who can tell me, did Jesus have anything to say about people who were given gifts or talents?'

There was a long silence. Everyone looked puzzled. Something wriggled into the back of Pippa's mind, something that had been said in Assembly by a visiting minister at harvest.

She didn't like to put her hand up, being new and that, but Miss Masters' eyes were everywhere. 'Yes, Pippa?'

'Is it . . . would it be the story of the men who were given talents and some of them didn't use them, and some of them did?'

'Good girl. Yes, indeed it would. Jesus told a story about people being given different amounts of money – or talents. Those who put their talents to good use were rewarded, but the person who buried his talent – that is, he didn't use it – was given the thumbs down.

'Now do you see what I'm getting at? Two of the

sisters used their talents not only for themselves, but also for other people. That's good. That's how Jesus wants it to be. But the third sister couldn't seem to do anything with hers; not only did she not use it for herself, but she refused to use it for other people as well.

'Now what does that mean to us, nowadays?'

'Not much,' said an older boy.

'Really? I didn't expect you of all people to say that! How about your talent for football? Aren't you currently starring in the first team at school?'

'Well, yes, but . . .'

'And aren't you taking part in a charity match soon? Isn't that using your talent for others? And your best friend David, sitting next to you, doesn't he use his talent for making things nice and neat? Doesn't he clean other people's cars?'

'But I keep the money!' said David.

'Well, now! You could have fooled me! I thought you used it for your bus fares to school, to save your mother's pocket. And Vibeke – and Pippa here – aren't you using your dancing talents to help other people?'

Vibeke said, 'But we're just enjoying ourselves!'

'You're using your talents to give other people a good time. You think that's not important? Believe me, it's as good as giving them medicine, like your father does. Making people feel better is definitely doing God's work.'

'You mean, being on the stage can be just as good as being a nurse or a doctor?' said one girl.

'Yes,' said Miss Masters. 'Cheering someone up is the same sort of thing. Think about it . . .'

Pippa did think about it. She hadn't thought much about Jesus before. Jesus was somebody your teachers told you stories about at Christmas and Easter. And there was a book in the school library that she'd read once, with good adventure stories about the people who came before Jesus in the Bible. She'd enjoyed that. But she hadn't thought that those stories could mean anything to her in real life.

Or not until now.

The story of the talents meant something to Pippa, especially the way Miss Masters had told it. Pippa understood that God had given her a talent for dancing. When she used it, she was happy, and when she didn't use it, she was miserable. That all made sense.

Pippa wasn't sure how using her talent for others was going to work out. But it was something else to think about.

And she'd never have known about it if Vibeke hadn't taken her along to church! Pippa realised that she loved Vibeke, perhaps more than anyone else in the whole world.

She was just so nice!

Chapter Seven

Miss Masters said, 'Now for homework tonight I want you to write about a story-book character. It could be Robin Hood or ET, or Aladdin, or anyone you've ever read about.'

A girl put up her hand. 'I'm going to the pantomime soon. Can I write about Dick Whittington?'

Pippa blushed and kept her head down. It hadn't occurred to her that anybody from school would be going to the pantomime, but of course it was the most likely thing in the world.

'Yes,' said Miss Masters. 'Anybody at all. Just get the facts right, that's all I ask.'

Pippa lifted her head and smiled at Miss Masters, and Miss Masters smiled back. She might even have winked. Pippa felt good. Her marks recently had climbed into the respectable range. She was holding her own at rehearsal, and she had something wonderful to look forward to. Life was good!

'Now,' said Ralph, the choreographer, 'we have to learn this one last dance. You're not bad in the villagers' dances and the wedding scene, and the hornpipe is coming along nicely. You only have to run around and squeak when you're playing at being rats, and the pageant scene is just walking about – but with your heads high, mind! No clomp, clomping!

'But this last dance is going to be hard. It's for the underwater scene. Dick Whittington and his friends have been shipwrecked and swim to shore through all the underwater creatures.

'The older chorus girls will be dressed all in black. They will move fluorescent fish around the stage in the dark. The audience will see the fish moving, but not the dancers behind them. And in front there will be the little waves and sea creatures – that's you. You will wear green leotards with filmy veils over them. Instead of doing the steps together, you will do them in sequence, one after the other, to make a rippling effect.'

Pippa couldn't understand what he was getting at, and to judge by the puzzled frowns around her, nobody else could, either.

He said, 'It is not as difficult as it sounds. Each of you moves on a different beat in the music, that's all. First we will listen to the music. There are eight beats in a bar. Listen . . .'

The music had a deep, well-marked beat, but the tune was smooth above it. Pippa thought, He means we've got to listen to the beat, and not to the tune, and *count!*

'Everyone will be lying flat on the floor at first. You will be in two lines diagonally across the stage, with numbers 1 and 2 in the front, and numbers 9 and 10 at the back. On the first beat numbers 1 and 2 will lift and wave and drop their left arms. On the second beat, numbers 3 and 4 move. On the third beat, 5 and 6, and so on. The effect should be that of a rippling wave. Let's try it, shall we?'

They tried it. Some of the girls got it right first time, but most didn't. Ralph was patient with them. He said he realised it was hard, but that they must COUNT! When one line got it right, the others were still floundering, but he moved on.

'We have a lot to do, still. Now I want you to form a circle facing to the left, with your right hands on the right shoulder of the girl in front of you. Lift your left arm, and sway in and out, in and out. . . . to a count of eight. You will be like a giant sea anemone, opening and closing. Now you walk round slowly in your circle, still waving your arm in and out for another count of eight . . . No, no, number 10. Your arm is too stiff!'

Pippa snatched a look under her arm, and saw that he was pulling and pushing at Carol, who had gone red in the face. Well, it wasn't easy. You really did have to count, or else!

'Number 2, watch your feet!'

Now it was Pippa's turn to go red.

The rehearsal continued till long past their usual time. Even Pippa was pleased to finish. They flopped down to change their shoes.

'I'm bushed!' said Vibeke, dropping her head down between her arms.

'Here, drink this,' said Marianne, holding out some hot soup from a flask to them.

'I can't eat at night, you know I can't!' said Vibeke, pushing it away.

'Your mother and I think you grow too fast for your own good,' said Marianne. 'So now we have a plan, and I bring you a little going-to-bed snack. Some soup, that I have made myself, not out of a packet . . . and some for Pippa, too.'

'I'll put on too much weight,' grumbled Vibeke, but she took the soup, and began to drink it.

'Mm-mm,' said Pippa. 'This is good. Why are you so

nice, Marianne?'

Marianne laughed. 'I am not specially nice, I think.'

'Yes, you are,' said Pippa.

'She's not!' said Vibeke. 'She bullies me from morning to night. Eat this! Drink this! Have you washed your hands? Have you done your homework?'

'I think she's nice!' said Pippa. 'Very, very nice!'

' "Very, very nice!" ' mimicked Vibeke.

Marianne put her arm about Vibeke, and hugged her. 'You are so tired, little one, no?'

'Yes,' said Vibeke, with an enormous yawn. 'I wish I could fall asleep right now.'

'Before saying your prayers?'

'Before washing, or undressing, or getting into bed or anything,' said Vibeke.

'Shall I have to say them for you tonight?' said Marianne, still cuddling her.

'Dear Jesus, if I've been bad today, I'm sorry,' said Vibeke. 'Please look after my daddy, my mummy and Marianne and help me learn this dance, Amen.'

Marianne laughed, but Pippa was shocked. She didn't know much about prayers. Until she'd been to church with Vibeke she'd thought prayers had to be serious. You asked God to bless people – whatever that might mean – and sometimes you asked for nice things to happen, like it not raining on Saturday. But you didn't joke about it.

She'd been twice to church with Vibeke, and prayers with Miss Masters were different, because Miss Masters asked each child in turn who or what they wanted to pray about. They prayed for poorly kittens, and friends at school who'd hurt themselves in the playground, and grandparents who were feeling a bit off colour, and things that had got lost.

That sort of praying brought prayer right into your ordinary life. Pippa had even started to pray a bit, herself, now and then. She didn't know if God would listen to her, because she'd hardly started to learn about him yet. But she thought it wouldn't hurt to tell him about the things that went wrong, just in case he did have time to listen.

But this was different. This was almost making fun of it.

'Pippa's shocked,' said Vibeke, sleepily finishing her soup.

Pippa said, 'No, I'm not!'

Marianne smiled at her. 'If there is only one thing that is sure and certain, it is that God loves children and wants them to talk to him and tell him their troubles and ask for his help and guidance. I don't think he will be cross with a tired little girl, just because she makes fun of things, do you?'

Pippa didn't know, so she just smiled and gave Marianne her empty cup. But when she went to bed that night, she whispered into her pillow, 'Dear Jesus, if I've been bad today, I'm sorry. Please look after Vibeke and Marianne and Tom and everyone, and help me learn that dance, Amen.'

Homework time. She had to get up early in the morning to finish off her essay.

DICK WHITTINGTON

A long time ago, a young man called Richard Whittington came from Gloucester to London. He came to look for his fortune. When he got to London he made friends with a cat called Tommy, and they decided to stay together. Later he found Alice, the daughter of

Alderman Fitzwarren, a rich merchant. Dick goes to work for the Alderman.

Dick has many adventures before he finally becomes the Lord mayor of London. Several times he runs away from London, but hears the bells calling him back, and he goes. His great enemy is King Rat who was the Lord Mayor once, but he was thrown into the Tower. He escaped and now wants to be Lord Mayor again.

One of Dick's adventures takes place when they all set sail on the Saucy Sal and King Rat causes the ship to sink, and they all end up in Morocco at the Sultan's palace, which is overrun with rats. Tommy helps Dick to get rid of the rats and then Dick has to fight with King Rat. He is helped by the Fairy of the Bells, who gives him a magic sword. Dick wins and King Rat is taken away by the Fairy of the Bells, to teach him to be good.

They all return to London and go to the wedding of Dick and Alice. Richard Whittington of Gloucester finally becomes Lord Mayor.

Miss Masters gave Pippa a special smile as she handed out the corrected homework. 'Well done, Pippa! I'm giving you an A.'

'Miss!' said Anita, holding up her hand, 'One of my friends that I play with, Kate, she's going to be in the pantomime at the Royal!'

'One of my friends tried for the chorus, but didn't get in,' said another girl. 'But we're all going to see it, anyway.'

'Good,' said Miss Masters. 'You might see someone else there who you know.'

'Who, miss?'

'Pippa is in it, too.'

'What?'

'Pippa the shrimp? I don't believe it!'

'Pippa is a talented dancer, and works very hard at it. So you see, we have our very own star in the class.'

Pippa blushed, and kept her head down. She thought the others might turn on her and tease her, but they didn't. Instead, they crowded around her at break time, asking her questions about the pantomime, and the dancing, and what Nita Yorke and Tony French were like, and could she get any autographs for them . . .

Suddenly she was popular. Three of the girls in her class wanted to walk home with her, including Janet! Lots more said they'd ask their parents if they could go to the pantomime to see Pippa dance. She could hardly believe it was happening to her, 'mouse' Pippa. Everything was changing because of the pantomime.

'Hi, shrimp!' said Tom. 'Come and see my new computer. It's given a whole new dimension to my life. It's brill!'

'Wow!' said Pippa. 'Can I have a go?'

'No, not yet. I've got to mug up on it first, and then perhaps I'll teach you later on. Don't touch that!'

'Sorry.'

Tom started hitting keys. His room was littered with discarded toys. His old games computer had now been pushed to one side on the floor. Pippa could remember when he got it. He'd promised to show her how to use it, but he never had done so.

'Can I have your old computer for games, then?' she asked.

'No, I've sold it to one of the boys at school. He's collecting it tomorrow.'

'Oh.' Pippa went downstairs. She was wearing her dance things under her anorak, and carrying her shoes in their bag. She went into the study, where her mother was wrestling with a sewing machine and yards of brown furry material.

'Mum!'

'Not now, dear. Can't you see I'm busy?'

'Yes, but . . . Mum, I need some new elastic on my ballet shoes. They keep slipping off when I jump.'

'Well, it'll have to wait. Tom needs to have his costume for the show by the weekend . . .'

Pippa reached for her mum's workbasket. 'Could I just take some elastic . . . ?'

'Hands off!' said her mum, slapping Pippa's hand away.

'But I thought I could ask Marianne . . .'

'I told you, I'll do it when I have time! I'm rushed off my feet at work, and now I've got to make this costume and I haven't done the weekly shopping list yet.'

Pippa was silent. She didn't think it likely her mum would have any time in the near future, and Madame had been making pointed remarks about children whose shoes kept slipping off, and holding up the rehearsal.

'Mum!'

'Yes, dear?'

'Did you get those tights for me, and the gloves and the four pairs of ballet shoes that have to be dyed to match our costumes?'

Mrs Fox hit her forehead. 'Oh, bother. I did mean to, but . . . I'll do it tomorrow. No, I can't tomorrow. At the weekend.'

'We've got the dress rehearsal next week.'

'Well, I'm sorry, but I've only got one pair of hands. Oh, bother. Now the thread's got in a tangle. I ought to stop. I'm making mistakes, but I've got to get this finished somehow . . .'

She pushed her hair back from her forehead with a tired gesture. Pippa was reminded of Vibeke, pushing her hair back from her forehead, and saying, 'I'm bushed!' or 'I'm pooped!' Vibeke had a different word for it, each time.

Once Pippa would have let it go, and perhaps gone off into a corner to cry, or run to Marianne to sort it out. But something was happening to Pippa. She had overcome all sorts of difficulties lately, and she wasn't quite so happy to be a doormat.

Also, some of Marianne and Vibeke's way of looking at things had rubbed off on her. Knowing a bit about Jesus and the way he loved people and wanted to help them, had something to do with it, too. Pippa had broken out of her old ways, and was beginning to notice when other people were in trouble. And if anyone needed help, it was her mum.

Pippa had never really listened before when her mum said she was tired. It just hadn't been convenient to believe it. Now she did.

Pippa said, 'I'm sorry, Mum. I've made a lot of extra work for you, haven't I?'

Mrs Fox sighed. 'It's not that I'm not pleased for you, darling, it's just that there never seems to be enough time to do everything that has to be done. Don't worry. I'll see what I can do about the tights. All right?'

Pippa remembered Marianne plying Vibeke with soup and chocolate to keep her going. That had worked a treat. Only, there wasn't any Marianne to do that for her mum. Or was there?

'Mum, shall I make you a cup of tea? I know how, honest.'

'Oh, would you, dear? Really? Can you manage? I must say, that would be nice. I don't want to stop in the middle of this . . .'

Pippa looked at the clock. She had a quarter of an hour before Marianne was due to pick her up. Pippa made a mug of tea, remembering exactly how her mum did it, and took it into the study. Her mum was back at the sewing machine.

Mrs Fox sipped the tea, and said, 'Thank you, darling. It's a long time since I had anyone to wait on me. I needed that. Tell me, are rehearsals going all right?'

'Yes. Look, Mum, don't worry about getting the tights and shoes and things. I know how busy you are. I'll ask Marianne if she can get them.'

'No, no. I'll do it.'

'It's just that Madame watches us all the time, and she said that if we weren't up to it, she'd put in one of the understudies. There's a friend of Carol's – she's the not very nice girl who leads our team – but this friend of hers is the First Reserve now, and she comes to all the rehearsals, and you can see she's just dying for one of us to get thrown out, so that she can get a place. And if I haven't got everything just right for the dress rehearsal, Madame might chuck me out.'

'I'll see to it, Pippa. I promise. I'll do the elastic on your shoes now, before I forget.'

When Marianne arrived, Pippa got into the back of the car with Vibeke.

'What's up?' said Vibeke. 'Have you got hiccups?'

'No. It's just that I was thinking how funny everything was, with us being in a pantomime with a cat, and Mum making a cat costume for Tom for his school play. But she did put new elastic on my shoes, and she said she'd get my gloves and things.'

'She's cutting it fine, isn't she?' said Vibeke. 'Mine have been done for ages. I caught one of my sisters trying to dance around in them yesterday. I was so scared she'd mark them. Luckily she fell over and hurt herself, so perhaps she won't try that again.'

Pippa wondered what it would be like to have younger brothers and sisters.

She said to Vibeke, 'Will you be my best friend? Just for the panto?'

'Sure!' said Vibeke. 'Why not?'

Chapter Eight

At long last they were able to have a run through on the stage with the cast.

The famous Nita Yorke was lovely with everyone. Although Pippa had been told that the stars usually kept to themselves, Nita would often pause to joke with other members of the cast, and even with the grown-up dancers. When everyone else was going hairless trying to get through a fast change of costume, Nita never appeared to be in a hurry, although she was always ready for her entrances. She even smiled and kept her temper when part of the scenery came loose and nearly fell on her. Nita was something else, and everyone adored her.

Tony French, playing King Rat, was also good-tempered. He knew his evil make-up might frighten the children, so he made a point of shaking them by the hand and talking to them in his normal voice before he went on stage and became all twisted and nasty. The kids loved him, too.

One of the odd things about a pantomime was that some of the women, like Nita, dressed up as men. The principal boy in a pantomime was always played by a girl. Nita looked smashing in her short, waisted jackets with their flared skirts. She had long, long legs ending in beautiful boots with tassels on them.

The other odd thing was that the chief funny lady was played by a big fat man. Donnie was a famous television comic, and he really enjoyed rolling around the stage as the Fat Cook, wearing a selection of fantastical bright clothes. He had a marvellous scene in which he undressed to get ready for bed, and all the members of the cast kept popping out from behind doors, under the bed and from inside the wardrobe, to interrupt him. He made everyone laugh, even at rehearsal, when there were only a few people to watch.

He had a special line in jokes, too. He'd tell the audience how everything had gone wrong with him that day, and how everyone he spoke to told him he was looking poorly. He wouldn't smile at all. Then he'd say at the end, '. . . but it's being so cheerful as keeps me going!' And everyone would fall apart with laughter. He was just great.

He was friendly with everyone backstage as well. Pippa and the other children had been told not to bother the grown-ups, and especially not to go begging the stars for their autographs, and they didn't.

But Donnie didn't even retire to his dressing-room when there was a hitch in the rehearsal, like the others did. One marvellous evening he showed some of the children a conjuror's trick. Pippa was on the wrong side of the stage and missed it, but she heard all about it, of course. She longed for him to speak to her, but the opportunity never arose, and she was too shy to talk to him of her own accord.

But one evening, when they were waiting for the lights to be adjusted, Pippa overheard him talking to the King of the Rats.

King Rat was asking Donnie why he always stuck to

comedy. Why didn't he try for some serious parts for a change?

'Not my style,' said Donnie. 'It's my job in life to cheer people up, not to make them cry. The way I see it, people often come into the pantomime feeling a bit down. Perhaps the weather's bad, or they aren't feeling too good, or they've got a lot of worries. The lights, and the glamour, the colour and the excitement all play their part in lifting them out of themselves.

'I've got my part to play in this, too. I make them forget their troubles by making them laugh. And they go home feeling better. "A cheerful heart does as much good as medicine," ' said Donnie, 'and I bet you don't know where that comes from.'

'You're wrong,' said King Rat. 'I have heard it before. In the Bible, isn't it? I wouldn't have sussed you out as a church-goer.'

'Well, that's where you're wrong, lad. I do go to church, and i read my Bible and I pray. It keeps me straight, and helps me to help others. Got it?'

Pippa was fascinated, and would have liked to have heard more, but just then they were called back on stage.

She told Vibeke about it, though. Vibeke was thrilled, because she'd always liked Donnie.

'You see, what Miss Masters said was right. Helping others to feel better is not only fun, it's doing good,' said Vibeke.

'You've helped me a lot,' said Pippa. She was too shy to come right out with it and say a proper 'thankyou'.

'Have I? Oh, by giving you a lift here? That's not much. I enjoyed it. You're always so nice to be with, no boasting or bad temper or anything. Not like some I could mention . . .' and Vibeke grimaced at Carol's back. 'And you understand about working hard and you dance so well. I really like being in the pantomime with you, because we can talk about everything that happens, and work on the hard bits together.'

Pippa couldn't put it into words, but she knew she wouldn't have been in the pantomime at all, if it hadn't been for Vibeke and Marianne. They had been so lovely to her, and there didn't seem to be anything she could do in return. One day, she thought, I'll find some way to show them . . .

Pippa had looked forward to the dress rehearsal, once her mum had got the right things for her to wear. But although it was fun wearing the bright new costumes, and very exciting to have the proper lighting on the stage with all the scenery, little things kept going wrong. Tempers were explosive.

Carol slapped the girl who was number eight, because she thought number eight had taken her costume, although she hadn't. Each child had a costume with her number on it, and of course they were graded in size from smallest to largest. Carol was growing fast, and she was finding her costumes a bit tight for her.

Some of the children's routines had been altered only the previous week when they got onto the big stage, and this was difficult, because they'd learned the dances one way, and now had to remember new steps.

Pippa liked the hornpipe best of all. They had snappy blue and white sailor costumes for it, with white gloves. They wore their tap shoes, and did a hornpipe on the Saucy Sal, just before King Rat arranged to have it sunk at sea. Then there was a quick change into their underwater costumes for the sea ballet.

The underwater ballet was the one which caused

them all so much trouble, because they had to time their actions to move in a wave, one after the other, and never at the same time. Also they had to run around the stage and take up new positions in the semi-darkness. No, it was not easy. But after a while Pippa found that if she stopped worrying about it, and just listened to the music, it wasn't impossible.

But half way through the dress rehearsal, a terrible thing happened. The Fairy of the Bells was played by a beautiful lady, who danced on her pointes and sang very high. Usually she was a bit of a giggler, but on this one particular evening nothing seemed to go right for her. The trap door wouldn't work and her costume split over the shoulders. She missed one of her cues, and that was bad enough. But real disaster struck in the pageant scene at the end of Act One.

The children were waiting for their cue in the wings. They were dressed as pages and ladies of the court. They had to walk down the steps with their arms extended, and big smiles on their faces. Unfortunately the steps they'd been practising on, weren't the same height as the ones on stage. Most of the children had to look down to avoid falling. Then it was the turn of the Fairy of the Bells. She had on a wide-skirted dress which was on the long side, and she tripped over it and fell in a sprawl!

Some of the children laughed. But the Fairy of the Bells didn't. She was furious! She started to tell the producer and the director and everyone what she thought of them and their stupid theatre . . .

Pippa blinked. She didn't like people being angry, and the lady was not only angry, she was using words that Pippa's parents would never allow, and some that Pippa had never heard before.

Suddenly Madame swept onto the stage from the wings, and said, 'Children – off to your dressing room, if you please!'

No-one argued with Madame. The children scampered off. Vibeke was laughing, but also a bit shocked. Carol said she'd heard words like that before, but she bet no-one else knew what they meant.

'That's enough,' said Madame, following them into their dressing-room. 'I've made it clear we will return when everyone is in a better temper, so take five minutes for a rest and a drink, and a visit to the loos.'

The director called her out into the passage, but the door didn't close properly, and Pippa heard him say, 'Madame, we can't have this sort of thing. You can't take the children off the stage just like that.'

Madame said, 'I'm not having my children exposed to smut or bad language.'

'Oh, but surely there's no harm in . . .'

At this point Madame realised the children could hear, and closed the door behind her.

'My money's on Madame,' said Vibeke. 'I bet Madame gets her to apologise.'

'What, a famous person like her apologise to a bunch of kids?' said Carol. 'Never!'

Pippa felt sick. What would happen if the lady did not apologise to Madame? Would Madame withdraw them from the pantomime? Pippa stroked her lovely tunic. She had a hat with a feather in it, too. When she and Betty led the others onto the stage and swept down the stairs, it was like . . . like floating. Surely nothing could stop it now, could it?

Madame came back into the room, smiling. 'Well, that's settled. The Fairy of the Bells is sorry if she upset anyone, and she's having a short break while they fix the trap door. Girls, we'll have to see if we can have a short practice with those steps before we leave . . .'

Pippa closed her eyes and said 'thankyou' to whoever was out there listening to small girls in trouble. She'd been to church with Vibeke three times now, and had found out a lot more about God, who loved children and who always listened to them. She was beginning to think that trusting in him made a lot of sense.

Chapter Nine

Pippa was having a nightmare.

'. . . and one and two and . . . lift those feet!' Madame was turning into King Rat, and he was chasing the children around the stage.

Pippa tried to wake up, but couldn't.

The rat was chasing her through the wings and out into the street, and she was screaming and running and running . . .

'Wake up, Pippa!'

Someone was calling her name. She was being shaken. She could hear them calling, but couldn't reply. Then the rat had vanished and she was wooshing her way up a dark tube and into the light.

She sat up in bed, breathing deeply.

'Having a nightmare, tots?'

It was her father, looking immense and hairy in his thick brown dressing-gown. He was smiling at her, but looking anxious, too.

'Mm.' She nodded, and smiled, and wiped her arm across her forehead. 'Being chased.'

'I know,' he said. 'What did you have to eat for supper? Cheese?'

'No, we didn't have time for anything much.'

Marianne usually brought something to rehearsal, but

that day she'd been held up at the dentist and they'd just had some chips that Marianne had bought round the corner. They weren't very nice, and neither Pippa nor Vibeke had eaten many.

'Well, how about some biscuits and a nice cup of hot milk?'

It sounded good. She pulled on her dressing-gown and padded down the stairs after him. It was nice being alone with him in the kitchen. He worked so hard that it wasn't often they had time to talk.

'How's the show going?'

'Great.'

'I hear you come home very late.'

'It's all right.'

'We've been worried about you, your mother and I. Thought you were a bit young to tackle a pantomime, and keep up with your schoolwork at the same time.'

'It's all right, honest.' She panicked a bit, wondering if he were going to forbid her to do it, even at this late stage.

'You do seem to be coping, I know. We're all very proud of you, you know.'

'Are you really?' That was nice.

'I've told everyone at work, and they say it takes a very special sort of girl to be in the pantomime.'

Pippa glowed. 'It's just that I like dancing.'

'And you're good at it, I hear.'

'You'll come and see me?'

'Try to keep us away. Most of the office are coming as well. Then there's Tom and all his friends, and all your mother's friends as well. I reckon we could buy out the whole house one night, just with the number of people who want to see you dance.'

She knew he was joking, but it was a nice sort of

joke.

'Oh, you!' she said.

'Seriously, though. We're all taking a larger size in hats, because of you.'

She grinned at him. 'Dad, I like being in the pantomime, of course. But I'm worried that I won't get to see Tom in his show. I'm in the theatre on the first night of his show, and that's when you'll be going to see him, isn't it?'

'Sure. We're proud of him, too. But I've got tickets for you and me, just the two of us, to catch his world-shattering performance on his second and final night.'

Pippa said, 'Will you really go twice? Just so that I can see him? Oh, that's really . . . magic!'

She tried to get her arms round him in a hug, but there was a bit too much of him for that. So he sat her on his knee, and that felt all right, too. She was beginning to feel more relaxed now, and leaned against him.

Something had been bothering her for a while, and perhaps this was as good a time as any to talk about it.

'Dad, you know that I've been going to Sunday rehearsals with Vibeke and Marianne . . .'

'We must find Marianne a special "thank you" present, don't you think?'

'Yes, that would be nice. But what I wanted to say was that . . . I didn't know if you knew . . . that we went to church on the way.'

'Yes, I knew. Mrs Cardoza asked your mother if it was all right by her.'

'And you don't mind?' She picked at the edge of his dressing-gown.

'No, of course not. You enjoyed it, didn't you?'

'Yes. I did. But I wasn't sure that you knew.'

'Well, we did. I'm glad you enjoyed it. It's something

we've rather lost sight of recently, being so busy all the time. Perhaps we could all start going again when this rush is over.'

'But Dad, could we go to Vibeke's church, do you think? Us children have our own time together, and it's Miss Masters from my school that looks after us, and well, it's not boring like staying in big church.'

'Like that, is it?'

'Mm.'

'Well, we'll have to ask the others, but I don't see why not. And will you stop unpicking my dressing gown, or I won't have anything to wear when I bring you down for your midnight snacks in future!'

That made her laugh. She had one more hard thing to say, though.

'You know, Dad, I shan't mind giving up the dancing lessons once the pantomime is over. Really, I won't make a fuss about it. It'll be so lovely to look back on it and remember.'

'Who said you'd have to give them up?'

'Well, but Tom's coaching . . .'

'And aren't you just as important in this family as Tom?'

Pippa blinked. She hadn't thought she was, no.

'Well, we've been talking about that, your mother and I. Having a job, keeping this house going and looking after two famous children is a bit much for her. So we're going to have an au pair to help out.'

'You mean, like Marianne?'

'I hope so, yes. We're bringing forward our plans to put heating in the top floor, so that we can open it up in the spring. Then you can have a room big enough to practise in, and the au pair can have a bed-sitting-room with her own bathroom.'

'Oh, that's . . . just brill!'

She hugged him again and again, till he complained that she'd got biscuit crumbs all over his dressing-gown. But she knew he didn't really mind.

She hadn't dared to think forward to what happened after the pantomime until now . . . but now . . . Now!

Life was frabjous, absolutely frabjous!

When she had first been picked to dance in the pantomime, Pippa thought the first night would never come. Each day dragged. Then had come the dress rehearsals and the trying on of the costumes, and getting shoes dyed to match each outfit, and the last minute changes and suddenly they had run out of time, and it was the first night!

Pippa tried hard to pay attention at school, but it was almost impossible. Her marks had been a lot better lately. She'd even found the lessons easier and had zipped through her homework in record time. Some of the things that had always been a mystery to her, like hard sums, suddenly began to make sense.

But today she simply could not concentrate. Miss Masters seemed to understand, because she didn't even get cross when Pippa stumbled over the bit of poetry she was reading aloud. 'Never mind, Pippa. I think we all realise that your thoughts are somewhere else today. The pantomime opened last night, didn't it?'

'Yes, Miss Masters. The A team were on last night, and we're on tonight. We do alternate nights.'

'Well, you'll have some friendly faces in the audience tonight, all cheering for you. I'm going with three of the other teachers.'

'And I'm going, too, miss!'

'And we're going next Tuesday . . . !'

'We couldn't get tickets till next month!'

Janet was jumping up and down in her seat. 'We're going twice! Once tonight, and once when my cousins come to stay in the holidays!'

'. . . and Mum's got a box, so the whole family can go!'

Pippa didn't know how to cope. This was Fame with a capital F!

'Thank you,' she said, and it sounded so comical that everyone burst out laughing, including Miss Masters.

'You're our very own little star,' said Miss Masters, 'so we'll forgive you if your head's in the clouds today, but woe betide if you're not back on earth tomorrow morning!'

'Oh yes, of course. I mean, I'm sorry if . . .'

'Sit down, Pippa!' said Miss Masters. 'Now let's get on with the lesson. Is there anyone else here capable of reading this poem through without getting stage-fright?'

Stage-fright!

Pippa felt a chill begin to grow in her tummy. What if she got on stage and got stage-fright? She never had done so before, but suppose it happened tonight, with everyone that she knew in the audience! It didn't bear thinking about!

She had to be at the theatre early, with her hair curled and her make-up on. Mr and Mrs Cardoza were taking so many people to watch Vibeke that they had no room for Pippa. Anyway, her mum said it was about time she learned the way to the theatre, so she took Pippa, leaving Tom to come later with his dad.

'This traffic is appalling!' said Mrs Fox, cutting up a lorry, and honking at an inoffensive cyclist. 'These roads get worse. Fancy digging up a sewer or whatever it is at a weekend! And look at that girl leaning right out of the car window! What on earth does she think she's doing!'

'It's Betty!' said Pippa, waving back. 'She's in the chorus with me. She's nice!'

'You think everyone's nice!' said her mum. They pulled up at the lights, and her mum tapped the steering wheel. 'I'm glad I don't have to do this journey every day. I hope you've got everything, because there's no way I'm going back, if you have forgotten anything.'

'No, I'm all right.'

'It's quite ridiculous, what they're paying you to appear in a professional pantomime. If I'd known . . . but as it is, it won't even cover the cost of petrol, taking you there and back.'

Pippa felt the brightness of the evening begin to ebb away. She'd been looking forward to it so much, and now her mum was spoiling it.

Mrs Fox patted Pippa's hand. 'Come on, now. Smile. I didn't mean it, you know. It's just my way, that's all.'

Pippa knew all about that. She nodded. Her mum was her mum, and they'd better both accept it. Her mum had a sharp tongue, and too much work to do, and sometimes she got a bit fraught. But she cared, all right. Look how she'd made time to buy and colour all those pairs of shoes, and curl Pippa's hair and even take her to the theatre.

'It'll be better when we have an au pair,' said Pippa.

'Yes, it will. I can't tell you how much I'm looking forward to that, even if it will mean having the builders in the house while we get the loft sorted out. Builders make so much mess! But yes, it will be nice. Sorry if I was a bit short with you. It's just . . .'

'Mm,' said Pippa.

They both knew what it was.

Mrs Fox leaned over to hug Pippa. 'You know, I'm so proud of you, I hardly know how to ... I keep thinking of when you were a little tiny tot, running around after me ... but you're growing up so fast ... one doesn't realise ... then one day you turn around and instead of a little girl, you're all dressed up with make-up on, and appearing on stage in the Theatre Royal ... and where's my handkerchief? The last thing I want is to catch a cold!'

The lights changed and they set off again. Pippa glowed. Her mum and dad really cared about her, and were as proud of her as they were of Tom! It was something Pippa had hardly dared to hope for, and it had happened. Pippa understood exactly what her mum meant about children growing up and changing without your noticing. She'd found that out with Tom, herself. And now her mum had discovered that she, Pippa, was also growing up, and was somebody to be proud of.

Pippa stopped feeling sick. She was not going to let herself have stage fright. She was going to enjoy herself. She was going on stage!

Chapter Ten

'Five minutes!'

The tinny-sounding voice came over the tannoy into the crowded dressing-room. Two adults, racks of costumes, make-up boxes and bags, shoes, tights, gloves, overcoats, anoraks, and ten children made quite a crowd.

There was a hasty peering into mirrors, and a fluffing out of skirts. The villagers wore pretty green and white dresses with bodices in a contrasting colour. The skirts stuck out, and were trimmed with ribbon.

Pippa's hands were sweating. She couldn't speak when Vibeke wished her luck. She just nodded.

The door flew open, and in came a messenger girl with ten posies in holders with frills on them. There was one for each girl! Everyone crowded round to grab their own posy. Pippa's was of white chrysanthemums, tied with green ribbons.

'But who . . . ?'

'Our parents, of course,' said Vibeke.

Pippa held the cool petals to her face. How marvellous it was to be loved. It made her feel a good inch taller.

'Overture and beginners, please!' said the voice over the speakers.

Betty shrieked. 'Where's my gloves! I've forgotten what we do first!'

'I feel sick!'

'You'll be perfectly all right,' said Madame, materialising just when she was needed, as usual. She gave them all a bright smile, and touched those she could reach. She told them they all looked lovely and that she was proud of them. Then she led them firmly out of the dressing-room, down the rickety iron stairs, across the greasy concrete floor, and into the wings.

The orchestra was playing Bang bang bang . . . or maybe that was Pippa's heart. She couldn't be sure. Betty and her four uneven numbered girls would lead on from the opposite side, but she, Pippa was responsible for starting off the whole pantomime from this side. If she tripped and fell over, what a disgrace . . . !

She felt panic begin to take over.

A large hand came onto her shoulder. She looked up into Donnie's brightly painted face, under its enormous wig.

And there behind her was Nita Yorke, smiling and swishing dust off her beautiful boots, and behind Nita was the cat, adjusting her mask, and the grown-up girls of the chorus, fluffing out their skirts and checking the ties on their shoes.

'It's a full house,' said Donnie, low down. 'Your first time?'

Pippa nodded.

'Ah. I've been watching you. You've got the makings, you have! So smile, girl!'

Pippa remembered. Helping other people to be happy did them as much good as if you were giving them medicine. She thought of all the sad people in the world. Could she really do something to help?

When I grow up, she thought, I'm going to do something to help other people.

The orchestra changed its tune, and the stage manager signalled to Pippa.

She threw back her head, picked up her skirts, smiled, and danced onto the stage as the curtains drew back and the lights came on. Betty came dancing out to meet her, but this wasn't their usual bouncing Bet. This was a frightened little girl, who had forgotten to smile.

Suddenly Pippa realised she'd been given a chance to pass on the love she'd received from Vibeke and Marianne. She didn't have to wait till she was grown up. She could do it now. She could help Betty.

'Smile, Betty!' Pippa gave the audience a dazzling smile, while whispering encouragement to Betty.

'Eek!' said Betty, trying hard to do so. Betty stumbled. She didn't seem to know what to do next. Disaster was about to hit the dancing line.

'Help!' thought Pippa. She grasped Betty's limp hands, and swung her round and round. Poor Betty had a look of complete panic on her face. Betty's hands were sweaty. Pippa could hear her breathing rapidly over the beat of the music.

'Into the big circles, skip to the left,' Pippa hissed. Betty nodded, and managed to release Pippa's hand to join up with the girls on the other side of her.

Now they were back in their straight line across the front, while the bigger girls came dancing on behind. Betty was picking up, but her smile still looked stiff.

The orchestra changed tune once more, and they all started to sing. 'London is a happy place . . .'

It was going to be all right. Betty was coping. The dresses looked fantastic under the lights. The dances were going well.

The children fell back to either side while the older dancers moved forward to their own dance routine. And that was when Pippa became aware of the audience.

It was breathing at her.

It was frightening. It was so huge out there. So black, but there were hundreds and hundreds of people, all watching, waiting to be amused.

For a moment Pippa felt fear touch her. Then she got a tiny wink from Vibeke, and she knew that Vibeke understood, and was trying to help her, as she'd tried to help Betty.

It was ALL RIGHT!

The audience liked them. Pippa could tell. She could feel that they were pleased.

It was a most exciting feeling. She had thought that dancing was the most exciting feeling you could have, but this was even bigger. She understood now what Donnie meant; cheering other people up was a good way to spend your life.

The pantomime proceeded. Pippa and Betty picked up confidence, but when it came to the change of costumes for the pageant scene, they grew tense again. Although Madame had tried very hard to get them more time to practise with the new set of steps, only the A team had had a second chance to use them. Carol said she hoped no-one would fall down them, and looked at Pippa and Vibeke with a sidelong expression that meant that she hoped they would!

Suppose they did trip and fall, as the Fairy of the Bells had done? It was all rather worrying, and they eased on their feathered hats, and white gloves, and checked over their appearance in the mirror without any of the usual excited laughter.

Betty and Pippa were to lead the chorus down the

stairs, and parade around under the supervision of the Fairy of the Bells, while Dick Whittington and his cat sat moping to one side. To add to the atmosphere of a dream, smoke would drift onto the stage from a machine at the back. They hadn't practised with the smoke, because the machine hadn't been working properly at the dress rehearsal.

The music signalled their entry, and Pippa and Betty stepped onto the highest stair and with glittering smiles, gracefully walked down the flight of stairs, and into the clouds of smoke. Betty's smile faltered. She almost disappeared in the smoke.

Pippa didn't like smoke, but she told herself that she wasn't really Pippa Fox any more. She was a romantic figure from the past, someone from a dream, beckoning Dick Whittington to come back to London, where fame and fortune awaited him.

She made it through the smoke, and turned to climb the stairs again, leading the others on and up. The Fairy of the Bells, also smiling, came down the stairs herself, rather more slowly than she had done the other day. The children paraded around and behind her, while Dick Whittington vowed that he would not be beaten, and that he would return to London. . . .

The curtain came down on a resounding cheer from the audience. The first half was over!

Vibeke hugged Pippa, who hugged her back, and Betty went around hugging everyone but Carol, who told her to go away and drop dead, little nuisance!

Then they all scrambled off to the dressing-room, only to find that Dick Whittington, the lovely Nita Yorke, had a special surprise for them on the B team's first night. Soft drinks had been laid on for them, and sandwiches, and just as they were getting changed, in she walked, with ten identical plastic bags with 'Dick Whittington' written on them. There was one for each of them!

Inside were balloons, and notebooks and sweets and a dinky little black cat. Nita even sat down with them, and gave them all her autograph on their programmes.

Pippa hadn't thought the children would have their names in the programme, but they did! There was her very own name, B Team, number 2 . . . Pippa Fox!

That programme was something to keep for ever!

Then it was queueing up to get to the loos, and into their sailor dance, with the snappy blue and white outfits . . . trying to stifle the clacking of their tap shoes as they crossed the concrete floor to get to the wings. The stage hands were sweating to get the new scenery in place, while the audience worked their way back to their seats, and the orchestra played the music to open the second act.

'All right?' Pippa whispered to Betty. For once they would enter on the same side of the stage, and this time Betty would have to lead them on in a long, tap-dancing line of 'sailors'.

Betty nodded. She was still a bit stiff with her smile, but her dancing was loosening up.

And on with the hornpipe!

Scramble off the stage, over the concrete, up the stairs, and into the babble of the dressing-room to strip off the blue and white of the sailors' outfits, and ease themselves into the clinging green leotards and filmy scarves of the underwater ballet. Each child had a real ostrich feather in her headdress, which floated and hovered as they moved. Green ballet shoes. . . .

On stage the 'boat' scenery tilted and sank as the stagehands manoeuvred it out of sight, and the lights changed to reveal the mysterious underwater world.

Pippa hadn't realised how good this scene would be. When they'd been rehearsing, it had seemed all very odd, with the older girls darting about holding cutouts of fishes and anemones. But now the older girls were invisible, and all you could see were the shifting green lines of the children as they stirred and tumbled and trailed their long green scarves over the ocean bed.

The music was thrilling, too. Weird and difficult to learn. But the children had been well drilled, and the waves tumbled and shifted just as they ought to do . . .

Then off stage to scramble into their rat costumes. Now that the difficult underwater sequence was over, they could relax and shout and laugh again. The rat costumes were heavy and hot, but it was great fun to squeal and pretend to bite and fight and then be chased all over the place by Dick Whittington and his cat.

And then off again, to rest for a little. It was hard work, being a rat. There was not much talk in the dressing-room, now. They got into their beautiful brocade costumes for the finale, changing shoes and gloves for the last time. The bigger children wore lovely tunics and hats, but Pippa and Betty had long red and gold dresses with little coronets on their hair, and big ruffs framing their faces.

Pippa looked at herself in the mirror, and blinked. Was that really her? She looked so different from her usual self.

Then onto the stage for the last sweeping appearance down the stairs, and across the stage, and the last happy chorus, and then the curtseying as the audience clapped and cheered and cheered again.

Pippa's face almost split with smiling.

This was the life! Perhaps when she grew up, she would be a dancer. Of course, she might grow the wrong shape, or suddenly develop an interest in banking or become an artist or want to be a pilot. She might. She thought now that she could do all or any of these things if she wanted to.

When she'd first been picked for the chorus, she'd been a timid little mouse, but she wasn't a mouse any more. The sky was her limit!

She didn't mind hard work. And out there was her family, all of them, her father and her mother and her brother, and she knew that she loved them very much, and that they loved her. And then there was Janet and her other friends from school, and Miss Masters too. Janet had asked Pippa to go round for tea as soon as the pantomime had finished. Pippa was looking forward to that.

She could cope with school now, because she had found herself and found something to work for.

And Jesus. She was going to go on finding out about him. She felt he would be happy that the people on the stage had done their best to help the people in the audience. Donnie was right. There must be lots of people in the audience who had come in feeling a bit below par, and were going away feeling a whole lot better.

'A cheerful heart does good like medicine . . .'

She'd remember that, always.

The curtain came down for the last time.

Vibeke threw her arms around Pippa, and hugged her. Little Betty came up and hugged them, too, so they hugged her back.

'Three more weeks!' said Betty. 'I can't believe it! Three more weeks of magic, and I never thought I had a chance!'

'. . . and next year, and the year after,' said Vibeke.

And Pippa said, 'Amen.'